WHAT REVIEWERS SAY
ABOUT DONALD HAMILTON

"Donald Hamilton . . . has brought to the spy novel the authentic hard realism of Hammett; and his stories are as compelling, and probably as close to the sordid truth of espionage, as any now being told."

—Anthony Boucher
In The New York Sunday Times

"Hamilton's sense of jaunty fun and a plot popping with sharp surprises are distinctive."

—Library Journal

"Hamilton writes tough, hard-hitting, action-packed novels that you simply can't put down."

—Doylestown, Pa., Intelligencer

"[Donald Hamilton] can write about the most horrendous happenings as casually as if he were asking for lemon with his tea."

—Martha Smith, syndicated reviewer,
Westchester County, N. Y., papers

"If you have half a dozen thrillers at hand and one of them is by Donald Hamilton, you can either grab it at once or save it for dessert. Mr. Hamilton is often novel, his pace is exemplary, and his capacity to divert spectacular."

—New York Herald Tribune

DONALD HAMILTON

MURDER TWICE TOLD

A FAWCETT GOLD MEDAL BOOK

Fawcett Publications, Inc., Greenwich, Conn.
Member of American Book Publishers Council, Inc.

DEADFALL

I

TWO men were waiting in the alcove outside the main office when Paul Weston came to work that morning. They had the briefcases and the neat, brushed, shave-shine-haircut-and-the-works look of salesmen, and he paid them no particular attention as he went past them and up the stairs. He had nothing against salesmen as long as they stayed out of the laboratory. He did not think of them again until an hour later, when Dr. Lowery, the chief chemist, came into the balance room where he was weighing out samples for analysis.

"Wes," Dr. Lowery said, beckoning, and abruptly Weston realized who the men must have been. There was only one thing Doc would take him aside to tell him with just that expression on his good-natured, aging face.

He put the weights back into the box at his elbow, closed the box, and closed the glass front of the analytical balance. Dr. Lowery waited for him outside the door.

"Mr. French wants you in his office, boy. Better put your coat on."

Weston saw the sympathy in the older man's eyes; and he did not have to ask the question and have it answered. He nodded, put his notebook away in his desk, and turned away, pulling off his acid-stained laboratory coat as he went into the locker room, which also served as reading room and reference library for the laboratory personnel.

The girl outside Mr. French's office downstairs said to go right in. Inside, Mr. French was waiting behind the big executive's desk. There was no friendliness or sympathy in his curt greeting. He did not ask Weston to sit down.

9

The two men Weston had seen earlier were sitting side by side on the maroon leather sofa under the photomural that showed the building in which they were, as it had looked when the sign ACME PETROLEUM CORPORATION across the front was bright and new.

As the door closed automatically behind him, shutting out the sound of the typewriters in the outer office, Weston became vaguely aware of the steady vibration caused by the paddles turning in one of the big mixing kettles down in the plant; and he remembered that he was supposed to be there when they shot the steam to it to bring the temperature up: nobody in the plant seemed capable of learning to read a thermometer. But the attitude of the heavy, well-dressed man behind the desk told him that it was not going to be any of Paul Weston's business if this or any subsequent mix got overheated.

Weston looked away from Mr. French to the two men on the sofa, regarding them with some curiosity. They always had the same look—when you looked closely—of trained competence. He had missed it this morning only because, after two years, he had no longer been watching for it. He wondered what happened if you kicked one in the face. Alcatraz, probably.

You would think there would be some kind of a statute of limitations on damn-foolishness, he thought bitterly. You would think that six desperate months of trying to find another job after being discharged from a government laboratory for keeping the wrong company, and a year and a half of hard work at the one he finally did land, would entitle a man to the right to kick himself in private for being a sucker for a girl with red-gold hair. . . . The men began to ask their questions. He said he had no idea where Marilyn George was. He said he had not seen her, or heard from her, since the day she had vanished, two years before, in Washington, D.C. He said he had no reason to think she was here in Chicago. Nobody in the room, he could see, believed him.

Then Mr. French took over, clearing his throat and saying heavily that he wanted to be fair; if there were any mistake here, he wanted to know about it. Otherwise,

Weston could understand that the company would not be needing his services after today.

"But I didn't know—"

He checked himself. Mr. French did not have a romantic nature. No reason you could offer, for having, even unknowingly, associated with the wrong kind of people, would be good enough for Mr. French. There were plenty of eager, stainless young chemists to be hired; there was no need for anybody to risk employing one who'd played around with a girl now wanted by the F.B.I. Mr. French clearly felt that there was no percentage in having people around who had been exposed to smallpox, leprosy, or sedition, even if they showed no immediate signs of breaking out in spots. . . .

Upstairs again, he found the door to the chief chemist's office open, and walked in. Jane Collis, Doc's secretary, was standing by the desk. Weston looked at her a little blankly, as if he had never seen her before: a small girl with medium-to-dark brown hair, a nice mouth, and glasses which she wore without apology so that after a while you forgot about them until she reminded you by having to wipe them, laughing, after you had kissed her. Well, it was tough about that, he thought.

A shiny quart sample can was her immediate reason for being there—Doc liked to pass on all customer's samples before Janie typed up the labels—but from the way the two of them had looked up when he entered, Weston knew they had been talking about him, waiting for him to return. He had told Dr. Lowery the truth when he applied for the job here, and Janie after he had started seeing her, off and on, in the evenings; long before he had bought her the ring that she was still not wearing by the terms of the agreement between them. The secrecy had been his condition, not hers. He was glad of it; it made him all square here if he could keep them from going out on a limb for him now.

Feeling their eyes on him, he grimaced and made a gesture as of a knife across his throat. You had to take these things with an air. A sense of humor was supposed to help.

"Oh, no!" Jane said softly.

Dr. Lowery asked, "Did French—?"

"My services are no longer required."

"I'll talk to him, Wes," the older man said. "For one thing, I'm supposed to do the hiring and firing up here in the laboratory—"

Weston said, "Never mind, Doc."

There was a short silence. Then Jane asked, "But what did those men want, anyway? Why can't they leave you alone?"

Weston shrugged. "I don't know. Routine check-up, I suppose."

"After two years?" Dr. Lowery frowned. "It seems a little unreasonable. You haven't . . . done anything that might . . . ?" He broke off, rather embarrassed.

"I haven't seen her or heard from her," Weston said, grinning abruptly as he understood what the older man was driving at. "Honest, Doc. I've been good; that's what hurts."

Dr. Lowery said, "I wasn't doubting you, boy. I mean, she might have tried to get in touch with you, or written you; that wouldn't be your fault. I just want to know the exact situation, so I know what to tell French when I see him. Maybe you'd better tell me the whole story from the beginning; I never asked you for the details. Just who was this girl you were mixed up with, anyway?"

Weston glanced at the girl by the desk; it was always a little uncomfortable to discuss one girl in front of another. "I don't really know," he said. "She called herself Marilyn George, but I gathered later that wasn't her real name. She worked in a government office in Washington. One day I had to get some stuff from that office for the lab where I was working, and she happened to be the one who looked it up for me. It was the beginning of a beautiful friendship." He made a wry face. "I saw quite a bit of her for a while; enough that I had a hell of a time later proving I hadn't slipped her any confidential information from the lab. I never did prove it; how can you prove a thing like that? They just couldn't prove I had, so I wasn't arrested, but of course they fired me on general principles. I had lots of company; apparently she'd had a collection of boy friends in strategic places, and some of them had made substantial contributions. That was proved. Naturally they wanted her testimony badly, but she got away from them."

Jane asked, "But didn't you suspect——?" and then broke off, coloring a little. They had never talked about it. It was just something he had told her because she had a right to know it; but he had let her know he did not want to talk about it. "I mean," she said awkwardly, "a person like that . . ."

"She wasn't any kind of person you'd think," he said. "She was just, well, a nice-looking kid with kind of reddish hair. She never asked me to tell her anything. If she had, I'd have told her to go jump in the Potomac." After a moment he went on, "Of course she had some half-baked political notions, but who the hell worries about . . . I mean, we didn't talk politics much."

The older man suppressed a chuckle. "Well, that's not important right now," he reminded them. "Let's remember that French had a valid point: it doesn't help the company any for the F.B.I. to be nosing around. But if Wes can show them. . . . You haven't been associating with anybody else who might have attracted their interest? You haven't joined any organizations, or gone to any meetings . . . ?"

Weston said, "Damn it, I've never joined a political organization in my life, Doc. Before, I was too busy earning my way through college, and then fighting the war after a fashion, to pay any attention to that stuff. And do you think I'd be fool enough *now* to get near any kind of radical outfit, even if I wanted to, which I don't? I mean, I hope I have a few brains, even though they don't always show." He grinned at them without amusement. "If I've been associating with any subversive characters, they're right here at Acme, Doc."

"What do you mean?" Dr. Lowery asked sharply, startled.

Weston was taken aback by the realization that, in his

position, he could not afford to make such remarks, even jokingly.

"I'm sorry, I was kidding," he said. "I just meant that everybody I know in Chicago, except for my landlady and a couple of bartenders, is right here in this building." After a moment, he said, "If nobody minds, I'd like to go look up those bartenders."

Dr. Lowery said, "Well, maybe it would be a good idea if you took the rest of the day off. I'll talk to French after lunch." Then he went on argumentatively, "It isn't as if he could claim you were dangerous here. Even if you *were* working with those people, what harm could you do here? We haven't any secrets that a good chemist couldn't learn in two days by analyzing stuff he can buy on the market. French certainly can't think you're going to set the place on fire or blow it up. When he calms down a little . . ."

Weston saw Jane Collis's eyes watching him, waiting to see what he would do. It annoyed him that she did not know that he would not let anybody risk more for him than Doc had already risked by giving him the job here. The trouble was finding a way to say what was necessary without sounding as if he were showing off.

"There's no sense all of us getting into this mess," he said. "Thanks a lot anyway, Doc, but let's just let it ride the way it is. . . . And if he doesn't know, you don't have to tell him you were aware of my history when you hired me."

Then he was out of the office. There was, for a moment, nobody in the laboratory outside and he looked it over with a sentimental feeling that he knew to be ridiculous: he wasn't that fond of the place. It was merely, probably, the last laboratory he would ever get to work in. The chances of finding another where somebody would give him the break Doc had given him here were infinitely small. Even Doc would probably never have risked taking him on, had it not seemed as if the thing were over and finished. It was one thing to take a chance on a man who had once been in trouble; it was something else again to help somebody who could be expected to keep the place cluttered up with agents of the F.B.I. He stood there for a brief time, slowly letting the full meaning of what had happened take hold of him, like a wounded man painfully visualizing a lifetime on crutches.

Jane Collis had come up beside him. He turned on her. "That goes for you too," he said.

"What?"

"You didn't know anything about me. I never told you a thing. Understand?" It was bad enough without anybody else getting dragged into it, particularly her.

The fluorescent ceiling lights flashed across her glasses as she looked up at him. She did not seem to have heard what he said.

"What are you going to do, Wes?" she asked.

"I don't know," he said. "Look, listen to what I'm telling you. I don't want you getting heroic about this, understand? Don't start shooting off your mouth to prove how loyal you are to me, or French will get the idea he's got a hornet's nest up here, and fire the whole outfit. Don't think he wouldn't, either. Just sit tight and pretend you never heard of me—"

"Will I see you tonight?" she asked.

"Tonight?" Then he remembered that they had been going to the movies.

He said, "I guess you'd better not count on me, Janie. I don't know what I'll be doing."

"Will getting drunk help anything?" she asked primly.

He grinned at her. "I don't know. I'll tell you when I come back for my stuff. So long, now."

"Wes." Her voice halted him as he was turning away. "Wes, can't I come with you?"

He glanced at her over his shoulder, and hesitated. The small girl in the plain skirt and sweater looked back at him steadily, but she was already, he found, a stranger. All he wanted from her now was the assurance that she would not be hurt for having known him. *Can't you understand that it's over?* he asked her silently, suddenly angry with her. *Can't you let me break clean?* He could feel it building up inside him like a head of steam. You never got used to having them lower the boom on you; there was always the impulse to strike back at somebody.

He checked himself; after all, it was not Jane Collis's fault that this had happened. Instead he shook his head and walked away; but at the locker room door he turned to look back at the small, not very striking figure moving slowly toward her desk by the windows. Looking at her only made it worse. He threw open the door, and there was a man at his locker, which was open. One of the laboratory technicians, a stout woman named Mrs. Neff, was watching the search with interest, a reference book forgotten on the table in front of her.

"That's my locker," Weston said softly.

The man, the larger of the two he had met downstairs, turned his head. "Just checking, Mac. Keep your shirt on."

The small room seemed suddenly to glow with white, shimmering light. Even Mrs. Neff had a halo—the only one, Weston thought, she would ever get to wear, the old witch. There were, he knew, some laboratory stands with a few spare rods tucked away behind the door. The rods were about the right size: half-inch bars of chrome-plated steel thirty inches long. He reached for one and heard Mrs. Neff gasp; and the man at the locker turned, his hand on the handle of the locker door.

"That's my locker," Weston said. "Close it and get the hell out of here. I'm tired of falling over you birds."

The man's mouth was open, saying something patient and reasonable but firmly insistent, even as the rod whined and Mrs. Neff screamed. The man did not get his hand back in time. The heavy metal bar caught him solidly across the wrist, and he sagged back against the lockers, gray-faced and limp with the sudden pain. Weston heard Mrs. Neff scream again, and realized that he was stepping forward with every intention of bringing the rod down across the bowed head of the larger man with every bit of strength he possessed; he checked himself with an effort that left him sick and blinded. *I almost killed him,* he thought. *I almost killed him!*

There was a step behind him. He did not turn, but let

himself be caught in an expert, disabling grip, not moving or struggling against it. In fact, he was grateful to it.

"Drop it," the voice of the second agent said in his ear.

The rod clattered to the asphalt tiles of the floor. The man behind Weston shook him a little, tightened the grip a little, hurting him experimentally to see if he could be made to resist; then released him.

"Just stand there," he said. "I don't want to see you move."

Weston stood motionless, watching the second man, somewhat smaller than himself and a little older, cross to his larger colleague. The two consulted together, the larger man displaying a wrist already turning blue and swollen.

Weston said, "There's a first-aid kit in the men's room, behind you."

"When we want advice from you, we'll ask," the man said sharply.

There were people at the door now. Janie was there, Weston saw, and Dr. Lowery, and the other technician —a kid named Bentley—with the morning's mail for the laboratory forgotten in his hand, and one of the girls from the office downstairs, and some guy from the plant in greasy coveralls. Weston could feel them looking at him as at something escaped from a zoo.

The big man turned to him, hugging the hurt wrist. "That was smart, Mac," he said scornfully. "That was really bright!"

Weston did not say anything. He had been told to be quiet.

"Can you think of any reason why I shouldn't have you arrested?" the man asked. There was perspiration on his forehead, but his voice was quiet. Weston remained stubbornly silent. He could feel nothing but a glowing hatred for the men in front of him, and for all the rest of them, whether he had ever seen them or not.

He was vaguely aware that the man in front of him was making a sincere effort to be objective, to understand what had happened so that he would not seem arbitrary or vengeful when he came to the decision he had to reach; but all this was a long way off, for Weston, and he stood there wishing only that the big man would make up his alleged mind and get the farce over with. *Trying to be fair,* he thought savagely, *now!*

"What the hell did you think it would get you?" the F.B.I. man asked, bewildered.

"Nothing," Weston said. "It's just something I've been looking forward to for a long time."

"There's no sense in your feeling like that. We're just doing our jobs. Sometimes we have to make trouble for people who perhaps don't quite deserve it, but we don't like it any more than they—"

"Then what are you doing here, mister?" Weston demanded. "If you don't like making trouble for people, why couldn't you give me a ring and have me meet you downtown somewhere? Or catch me when I came home from work? No, you have to march into the place with horns, bells and whistles, letting everybody from the president on down know—" He choked on his anger. "Just too lazy or thoughtless to think what it would do to me! The same damn questions you asked me two years ago, and they can't wait until five o'clock tonight; no, you've got to have me called into the front office to answer them! Like little tin gods, just because you've got badges—"

He turned abruptly to the still open locker, put his hat on his head, and went out carrying his topcoat. Some of the pressure had been relieved, but there was enough left to make him hope that somebody would try to stop him. Nobody did. It was dark on the stairs and there was weak fall sunshine outside. He took a month's wear from the recapped tires, sending his battered secondhand car away from there. Nobody came out after him.

II

It was well after dark when he found himself in a little bar off the lobby of a big downtown hotel, the name of which seemed familiar although he had never been in the place before. It was one of those hotels. He knew that he was quite drunk, perhaps a little drunker than he had ever been in his life, but he was still navigating with reasonable accuracy, speaking with sufficient clearness to be understood by the bartenders who confronted him; and the liquor was not helping him to forget anything. He knew that he was getting drunk mainly by the fact that he kept feeling more and more sorry for himself. It seemed to him that he had behaved very creditably throughout the whole affair, not losing his temper once until today, not changing his name or lying to anybody or concealing anything; and if you did it that way, and they still wouldn't leave you alone, what hope did you have of ever getting clear of the mess? He never knew how long the girl had been standing beside him when she finally spoke, asking him for a light.

Something in her voice stirred a memory inside him. He turned his head to look at her and saw her smile at him politely. She was a moderately tall girl with short light hair brushed into a feathery halo about her head. An elaborate dress, almost long enough to be an evening gown, of a stiff, blue-black, iridescent material like taffeta, rustled when she moved; it was pulled back into a ridiculous bustle in the rear.

"Please?" she said, holding her cigarette steady in front of him.

"Certainly," he said, and lit it for her, then turned back to the bar, a gentleman, not taking advantage of the favor he had done a lady to force his acquaintance on her. Her dress whispered beside him as she, also, turned to the bar. He felt his heart begin to pound as he waited.

After all, you could cut short the long untidy mane of red-gold hair and let it revert to what was probably its natural color; you could exchange the clothes of a rather careless, underpaid young government clerk for those of a fastidious, well-to-do society girl a few years older; you could even, if you were doing the character well, train and diet the young body to a more fashionable slenderness and the face to a more striking gauntness, but the blue-gray eyes would remain the same, and the short fine nose; and the long mouth would never be changed, for anyone who had known it well, by any subtleties of makeup or expression. Meet her anywhere, with any clothes or name she might choose to wear, and she would still be Marilyn George.

He was not so drunk that he did not know quite well how it would look to anyone seeing her beside him, after he had just finished swearing that he had not been in touch with her for years. He had no doubt that she was quite aware of this, and had come deliberately to incriminate him by her presence, as part of some game she was playing. It was clear now that the F.B.I.'s visit to the plant that morning had been part of something bigger than just a routine check-up. Whatever the situation, there was obviously nothing to be gained in trying to shoo her away from him now; and a man trying to avoid a good-looking girl was invariably a ridiculous object.

"I wondered if you'd recognize me," she said without looking at him.

He could see their two faces in the mirror, neither looking directly at the other. There was no point, he reminded himself, in bitterness or recrimination. She knew what she had done to him; and she felt the way she felt about it, however that might be. Nothing he could say could get him any more than pity from her; he probably could not do better than a kind of contemptuous sympathy.

He had a momentary thought of Jane Collis, who still had his ring; but the kindest thing he could do to Janie would be to get out. He stood there at the bar, getting a small, mean satisfaction out of letting the girl beside him do the work of picking him up, knowing that he was going to follow her lead at least until he could see what she wanted. He remembered that there had been a time when he had wanted to kill her. . . .

In the morning he could not remember at once where he had left the car and this worried him, because he would need what little he could get for it when his savings ran out. Then he remembered parking a block and a half up the street; they had walked the remaining distance with great dignity, trying to impress each other with their complete soberness. He focused his mind on the building they had entered and it came back to him hazily: one of those gold-plated apartments near the lake front that sported a doorman, like a hotel.

"Paul," she said, shaking him.

Nobody had called him Paul for a long time. It was a name he had left behind, with some other things, when he left Washington two years before. Paul was one kind of person and Wes was another; but somebody apparently did not know the difference.

"Paul, wake up."

He opened his eyes and looked at her. She did not look the way he felt; she was dressed in a tailored blue robe of some light woolen material faced with satin like a man's dinner jacket, and she looked very slender and young and freshly awakened—until he sat up stiffly, and his vision cleared, and he saw that she did not look quite as good as all that. Not *bad,* he thought, *still not bad at all.* But no chicken, now. Well, he was two years older, himself.

"Eggs sunnyside up or over?" she asked him, smiling.

"Up," he said thickly, not quite awake yet.

She said, "The john's through the bedroom. There's a razor in the medicine cabinet. And you don't have to walk all over my mink coat."

He stood up clumsily, pushing his shirt back into his trousers, and faced down the expensive modern living room that was not the kind of room to encourage intoxicated men to fall asleep on its pale sofa with their shoes on. He looked at Marilyn George and remembered a way he had had of thinking of her: hunted, fleeing, walking the streets in run-over shoes and snagged stockings, like him looking for a job where nobody would question her past. . . . Well, he thought, it was always surprising the number of ways you could be wrong. He picked up the glossy fur coat with which she had apparently covered him when he passed out, laid it gently on the sofa, and went out without looking at her again.

When he came into the kitchen, shaved and fairly presentable, with an aspirin taking the edge off his hangover, she had breakfast ready in the gaily painted breakfast nook; she served them in silence and they sat facing each other across the table, eating, at first, without conversation. From where he sat he could see all of the small kitchen, with a back door opening on an iron fire escape. Everything in the place looked as if it had just been installed.

Last night they had had a fine time playing a game of pretending that nothing bad had ever happened between them; but it was morning now.

She looked up and said abruptly, "In Washington . . . I tried to keep you from being involved, Paul. You won't believe that, but it's true."

He studied her face and, after a moment, shrugged and went on eating. "Well, it's not really very important now, is it?"

"It is to me," she said. "I know you think I deliberately . . ."

He buttered a corner of toast. "Look, Marilyn," he said, "it was two years ago and to hell with it. I'm not worrying about what you did to me two years ago. I'd just like to know what you're trying to do to me now."

She glanced at him sharply.

He said, "Let's assume that I'm reasonably bright, even if it's a strain. You didn't pick me up in that bar last night just by accident. You didn't even do it all by yourself. You hadn't trailed me through the places I'd been before I got there, not in the outfit you were wearing. Somebody spotted me for you, and when I was in position, suitably tight, you moved in. Am I right?"

After a moment she nodded.

He said, "All right. Make the proposition."

"What do you mean?"

"Come on," he said impatiently. "You didn't bring me here to make love to me, and you didn't bring me here to feed me. You brought me here because just by being here I convict myself of being a liar and probably a traitor—"

"And you came anyway?"

"What have I got to lose?" he asked. "It's a cinch I'm never going to get another job in chemistry with the F.B.I. turning up to haunt me every few months. I played it straight once, right out of the boy scout manual. They walked right in and loused it up for me. Now I'm making my own rules. What have you got to offer?"

He watched her rise and bring the coffee from the stove to refill their cups. She was, he noticed, really quite a bit thinner. When she sat down again, her fingers went nervously about lighting a cigarette. Something about the gesture seemed to add a couple of years to her age.

"Paul," she said, "just how do you feel about . . . about the people I work for?"

He shrugged his shoulders. "I never bothered with politics much, if that's what you mean." He was not in a position to indulge in high-flown phrases about right and wrong.

"Then if somebody offered you some money to—?"

"How much?"

"A thousand dollars?"

"You can't live very long on a thousand, these days."

Something changed in her eyes. She crushed out her cigarette and rose, turning away from him. "You'd better talk it over with a friend of mine," she said. "I'll make the arrangements." She went quickly out of the room.

He finished his coffee. His brain felt thick and useless; he had been trying out an attitude, trying to come to a decision about it, but he could not see the answer clearly. It was easy enough to use the words *spy, traitor,* but what did they mean, after all? How many times did you have to get kicked in the teeth before you were entitled to switch your loyalties somewhere else?

He rose and walked into the living room. She was standing by the alcove of windows at the far end. He came up beside her, and they stood looking out at the steady fall rain dripping into the park across the street. Somewhere facing the same park, Weston remembered, was Jane Collis's tiny kitchenette apartment. He put the thought aside, and watched the cars pass along the glistening asphalt drives down there, drives that looked more like water than the flat gray surfaces of the ponds and winding lagoons, now roughened by the rain. Beyond the park you could see the lake, but there was no horizon.

"I didn't hear you telephone," he said.

She did not look at him, and her voice was barely audible. "Maybe I don't want you to—"

"What?"

She shook her head mutely, then turned suddenly to look at him, and they faced each other for a moment. Then he put his hands on her narrow waist, and her hands dropped to his wrists as if in protest, but she made no effort to free herself beyond that, and when he drew her toward him she came forward obediently, and her lips were alive to his kiss.

He stepped back and wiped the lipstick from his mouth, turned, and walked away from her to the telephone stand in the little front hall. Her voice followed him, puzzled.

"Paul, what—?"

He looked up a number in the book. When he reached for the phone she was beside him, her hand holding the instrument down. She looked at the U.S. Government listings on the open page, and her free hand came out of the drawer below the telephone, holding a .320 Colt aumatic pistol.

"Don't," she said quietly. "Get away from the phone."

The gun did not go with the apartment, nor with the slender hand that held it. There was nothing expensive or feminine about the weapon; it was Mr. Colt's stock model in that caliber, without radio, defroster, or white sidewall tires. It would not give good FM reception, change the baby, or make you attractive to the opposite sex. It wasn't, Weston thought, even much of a gun. You would starve to death before you filled the pot with what it killed, even in a country teeming with game. When you came to think of it, the object was practically useless. It wasn't good for a damn thing except shooting a man at close range.

"You didn't have to kiss me," she whispered.

He started toward her. She should not have done it, he thought, she should not have given him this opening; it was unfair. He had tried to keep the whole thing on a reasonably civilized basis, in spite of what he owed her, and then she started making with guns. It was stupid. It was ridiculous. She began to back away from him, her shoulder brushing the wall. She came to the alcove in the corner and was brought to a halt by the sofa beyond. He walked up to the weapon until it bore against his chest, feeling very brave. Then he put his hand on it and turned it gently away from himself. He brought his other hand up and disengaged her fingers from the butt. Then, suddenly sick and trembling inside, he knocked her down with a full arm-sweep of the hand that did not hold the gun.

"Next time you try that," he breathed, "you two-bit Mata Hari, I'll ram the damn thing down your throat butt-first!'

He did not recognize his own voice. After a moment he turned away and went back to the telephone and dialed a number, dropping the gun into his coat pocket. Presently he was aware that she had left the room. A man's voice spoke in his ear.

He said, "Two of your agents were at the Acme Petroleum Corporation yesterday. One has a bum wrist. I'd like to talk to him if he's around."

He was told to wait. After a considerable time, the voice of the big man he had struck in the locker room said, "Richardson here."

Weston said, "This is Paul Weston. I want to tell you where Marilyn George is."

"You're a little late, Mr. Weston. We've had our eye on her ever since you made contact with her last night."

Weston said, "I don't give a damn where you've had your eyes. I'm merely going on record as reporting that— take it down and mark it from me—Miss George is at the Shore Arms Apartments, apartment 608N." The number was on the tag of the key that still lay on the little stand where she had dropped it as they came in the previous evening. "That's the north wing of the building. You turn right as you come in the door." The anger that came when he even thought of them was sour in his mouth. He could not keep it out of his voice. "You came around and asked me," he said. "You made a big show of it. It was important enough to get me fired for. Well, now that I know, I'm telling you. I don't want to hear, later, that I'm in trouble for keeping it a secret."

The man called Richardson sounded unimpressed. "All right, Mr. Weston, you've reported it. Anything else?"

"Yes. She wants me to meet a guy. A sum of money has been mentioned. Shall I go?"

There was a space of nothing. Then: "Where is Miss George now?"

"In the bedroom with a sore ear," Weston said. "She had some objection to my calling you."

"In other words, she knows you're talking to me?"

"Hell, she's probably listening."

"I don't understand, Mr. Weston. Are you asking my permission—"

Weston said clearly, "You're a representative of my government, God help it. As a good citizen, I'm notifying you that somebody has made me a questionable proposition. I'm asking you whether to go ahead with it and see what these people want, or tell them to go to hell."

"And the girl is listening to you asking?"

Weston said, "For all I know, the damn place is wired for sound. Just answer the question: do I say yes or no?"

III

When he came into the bedroom she was lying face down on the big bed, crying.

He said, "All right, I've seen you, Marilyn. You can turn it off now."

She moved her face a little from side to side against the pale blue satin coverlet, rumpled now and stained with tears over the pillow. He sat down beside her, for some reason that was not quite clear to him. There were times when you had to make it up as you went along; he had hit her and now he was sitting down to comfort her. It did not make sense, but then, nothing else did, either.

"I wouldn't have shot," she whispered, her voice muffled. "You knew perfectly well I wouldn't shoot. Why did you have to hit me?"

He lifted her by the shoulders and, after a moment's hesitation, she turned to him and buried her face in his coat.

"I'm sorry," he said. "I don't know what's been getting into me lately. That's the second time in two days I've gone up in blue smoke. I'm sorry as hell, Marilyn."

She shook her head minutely. "No," she gasped, "no, you're not; not really, and that's the terrible thing, because you were such a nice boy. . . ." He winced. "You were," she breathed. "You were so sweet, and you wanted to make me so happy, and you were kind of cocky and proud of me when we went out together. And now you knock me down with your fist," she said, "and don't even bother to see if you've hurt me."

"It wasn't my fist," he said. "Anyway, I've said I was sorry."

She said, "It's not that, it's just . . . Sometimes you see things you've done to people and wonder . . . if there's really any excuse for you. Particularly when you no longer believe . . ."

"Believe what?"

". . . believe in what made you do it in the first place," she whispered, her breath warm against his throat. "I'm glad you called them, Paul. I had to try to stop you, but I'm glad."

She lifted her head to look at him. He gave her a large white handkerchief and watched her use it.

"That's kind of a quick conversation," he said quietly. "Marilyn, who do you think you're kidding?"

Her voice was suddenly sharp. "What do you mean?"

He said, "You didn't feel this way about it last night, when you made contact with me deliberately to tie me up tight with your lousy outfit. You aren't going to claim you were trying to be inconspicuous in that little taffeta number, are you?"

She got slowly up from the bed without looking away from him.

He said, "As I see it, somebody needs me for something. This guy wanted to have something on me, so that if I balked at what he wanted me to do he could point out, oh, so politely, that I didn't really have any choice. Who's going to believe that I just happened to run into you in a bar last night? Or that I passed out on the sofa here, if that matters? After coming up here, what chance have I got to prove that I'm not part of the gang, particularly when a couple of witnesses can probably be supplied, if necessary, to testify that I've been working with them right along. . . . Is that what you're building up to, Marilyn, to confess everything to the F.B.I. including a couple of facts that don't happen to be so?"

She said stiffly, "Go on."

He said, "Well, that's out now, Sweets. For the moment, I'm in the clear. I'm not your accomplice; I'm still an innocent bystander trying to act like a good citizen. Sure, I spent the night with a girl I used to know in Washington, but the minute I sobered up I remembered that she was wanted and reported her. You can't turn me in, darling, because I've just finished turning you in. I've even offered to risk my life finding out what your game is. They don't have to believe me—they probably don't—but if they're reasonably honest they're going to treat me carefully until they can prove I wasn't acting in good faith. As a matter of fact, the man I talked to more or less gave me authority to go ahead; he couldn't very well refuse and have me claiming that they weren't only persecuting me, they were even forbidding me to make any move toward finding evidence to clear myself." He grinned without amusement. "So your boy friend hasn't got anything on me. He can't turn the screws and watch me squirm. I'm not part of his outfit unless I want to be; hell, I'm working for the government. So now I'm willing to listen to his proposition."

He looked up at her, waiting for her to speak, and found himself realizing that you never really got over it: once you had been truly in love with a person, that person always retained a certain power over you. It was this, and not the reaction from being threatened with a gun, that had made him strike her, fighting against the knowledge that her kiss had stirred him in a way a hundred Jane Collises never would. It was this that was making him do his best to hurt her. It did not seem quite fair that he should have to sit there looking at a girl he had every reason to hate and feel disturbed by her thinness, worried by the small signs that kept cropping up to show that her nervous system had been taking a terrible beating. What was it to him if she was becoming bitter and disillusioned; did he want her to be really happy in the line of work she had chosen for herself?

She said, quite softly, "I wouldn't, Paul."

"Wouldn't what?"

"Whatever you're trying to do. Either way, you're double-crossing somebody—us or the others—and you're not smart enough, or tough enough, to carry it through. Why, if you had what it takes to do that, you wouldn't be sitting there looking ashamed of yourself every time you happen to notice the bruise on my face!"

He got up. "That's all right," he said. "I'll struggle along as far as I get. Thanks for the advice, though."

After a moment her shoulders, slender in the tailored blue robe, moved in a shrug. "Well, that takes care of my good deed for today. If you'll get out of my bedroom I'll get dressed now."

He started to pass her without speaking. Making way for him, she seemed to stumble, her heel catching somewhere so that she fell against him. Then her arms were tight about his neck, holding him.

"Get out of here, you stubborn idiot! Who do you think you are, Dick Tracy? Get out, get out, get out!"

For a moment he believed her. Then, not quite sure that his first instinct had not been right, he knew that he could not take the chance: she could be only testing him. Something in her attitude had been calling for his attention, and he pushed her away and said deliberately, quite loudly:

"So the place *is* wired for sound. The only times you've dared talk straight is when you've had your mouth right up to my ear."

Her face paled a little, and he saw her glance shift to the head of the bed, and back to him. She stepped back and drew herself up.

"That wasn't a very nice thing to do to me," she said quietly. "I was trying to help you."

He said, "I remember how you helped me once. Let's make with the phone, huh?"

IV

When he returned to the apartment house that evening, after going home to change, he could not find her name on any of the polished brass mailboxes in the lobby. He stood there, feeling helpless and quite ridiculous, until he remembered the apartment number. The engraved card in the slot opposite this number displayed the name of a Mrs. Elaine Susan Beckworth. He shrugged and pressed the button anyway, and the buzzer admitted him to the elevator. She had the apartment door open for him, and was in the living room mixing a drink when he came in. Her evening gown was of smoky blue-gray chiffon that seemed to drift about her quite weightlessly as she turned to greet him. He took the glass from her hand and examined her appearance critically, witholding his approval for a calculated time. Her eyes, he noticed, were a little too bright, and her cheeks were flushed; she must have had a couple of drinks alone while waiting for him. Or perhaps she had had other company while he was gone. He put aside the thought of the other men she must, in her business, have known—with an effort.

"You look as beautiful as in a dream I once had about you," he said. Then he spoiled the compliment deliberately by glancing at his watch, which read almost eight-thirty. "Let's get this over with, shall we?"

"We have plenty of time," she said. "What happened? In the dream?"

He glanced at her. "When I tried to reach you, something fell on me. I woke up."

"You made that up," she said calmly. "You never dreamt that."

"No," he agreed. "But I might have, mightn't I?"

After a moment she turned abruptly away from him, putting aside her half-finished drink. "Maybe we'd better go," she said.

He watched her cross the room, knowing that he had hurt her. There was no satisfaction in the knowledge, any more than there had been in striking her. It was like getting mad and driving a fist at the wall. You could make a dent in the plaster, all right, but it was your own knuckles that bled. She waited for him at the apartment door. A length of the blue-gray chiffon was drawn about her otherwise uncovered shoulders like a fragile shawl, the ends passed through a small gold ring to hold them in front. She wore no other wrap.

"No coats?" he asked.

She smiled, deliberately mysterious. He shrugged and followed her into the elevator, and watched her push the

31

button for the floor above. He thought he should have known it.

A tall man in dinner clothes was awaiting them on the seventh floor landing, the apartment door opened behind him. He was quite blond, balding, and there was a small scar under the corner of his right eye. For some reason the scar gave the impression of having been caused by the excessive kick, backfire, or explosion, of a rifle; perhaps because the man had a rifleman's eyes. They looked at one object at a time, able to disregard everything else.

Marilyn introduced the two men, and they shook hands. Weston made no attempt to match the other's grip; it would not have done him any good to try.

"I'm very glad you could come, Mr. Weston," said the man, whose name was Louis and, apparently, nothing else. "I'm always delighted to meet any friend of Elaine's."

Weston looked around for Elaine, a little startled, before he remembered the name on the mailbox downstairs. He reflected that Marilyn must have fun trying to keep her various identities apart. There was something childish about this business with names that gave him a little confidence. He murmured a polite phrase about being overjoyed, and Marilyn led them into the apartment, which was in all respects, even to the furniture, a duplicate of the one below. Only a few details were different: a hunting print in the place of a watercolor, a pipe rack and humidor in the place of a cigarette box and lighter. Beyond the archway that divided the living room from the dining room a table was elaborately set, waiting for them. A boy in a white coat was filling the water glasses.

Weston found himself a little puzzled by the whole performance; then he understood that these people, leading the lives they did, would naturally seize what opportunities they could to impress others with their polish and respectability: it was a form of compensation. Louis clapped him on the shoulder.

"Did you expect to find a couple of sinister characters peering at you by the light of a candle stuck in the neck of a bottle? Speaking of bottles . . ." The tall man glanced sideways as they all crossed the room toward the sideboard. When he spoke again, his voice was a little diffident, as if he were calling Weston's attention to a point of local etiquette with which the new man could hardly be expected to be familiar. "I say, Weston. That gun you're carrying, fella. I mean, how about parking it out in the hall, hunh? Just as a favor?"

Hesitating, Weston was aware that the bedroom door, to his right, had moved a little as if someone behind it had brushed it, changing position. Well, it was hardly likely they were going to shoot him here, he thought. He faced the tall man, deliberately turning his back to the slightly open door.

"I mean," he said, "if you want it, how about taking it away from me?"

The challenge sounded brash and melodramatic in the pleasant surroundings. There was no check or break in the tall man's movement as he arranged the glasses before him on the sideboard and reached for the martini pitcher. He did not even look up. But you could sense a certain tension.

"I can, you know," he said mildly.

"I know you can," Weston said. "But is it worth the trouble? You might even have to shoot me; and I'm no good to you dead." He did not turn his head or change the sound of his voice. "Marilyn, you're going to get an elbow . . ."

When a person stepped behind you at a time like this there were two good explanations for the act: they could be preparing to help disarm you, but they could also, unlikely as it might seem, be trying to shield you from the fire of a gun aimed at your back. . . . The thought gave him a momentary pleasure, but he called himself a fool. There was no decision to be made, because the treatment was the same in either case.

The man in front of Weston inclined his head slightly, and the girl behind Weston moved away.

Louis smiled. "All right. If you feel so strongly about it, we'll pass the gun."

"Is that a bargain," Weston demanded, "or do I order a rearview mirror to see what she's up to now?"

"It's a bargain."

Weston studied the long, pale, rather handsome face for a moment. Then he took Marilyn's little automatic pistol from his pocket and laid it on the sideboard and grinned.

"The script was strictly horse-opera," he admitted. "I wouldn't know what to do with the gadget if I did have to use it." He glanced at the girl standing by the fireplace now. "I just wanted to see which way the outlying counties would vote."

She raised her head a little, startled.

He said, speaking to her directly, "Stay out from behind me. Stay where I can see you if you want to stay pretty."

"There's no need for threats, Weston," Louis said reprovingly.

"No," he agreed. "Give the lush her drink and let's—"

"That's enough!" The tall man stepped forward, annoyed. Marilyn's face was quite pale. She did not move.

There was a certain pleasure to be had from knocking the props out from under all this fake gentility, whatever the reasons for doing it: whether he was punishing her for betraying him or shielding her from the consequences of trying to help him. He did not know which, and something inside him needed to keep hurting her.

"Well, that's what she is, isn't she?" he snapped. "Look at her—she's been tanking up all afternoon. It's a wonder she can still—"

"I said, enough!"

There was a brief silence. Then the tall man chuckled with sudden understanding.

"I see," he murmured. "You really thought she'd back you up, didn't you?"

"She backed me up, all right," Weston said bitterly.

After dinner, the boy in the white jacket brought them coffee in the living room. Louis spoke casually over his shoulder, telling somebody to get himself something to eat, and a short, square man in a threadbare brown suit came out of the bedroom. While the door was open, Weston caught a glimpse of a machine resembling a dictaphone in the far corner of the room, presumably the receiving end of the microphones downstairs. He made a gesture in that direction as the door closed and the man in the brown suit went on into the kitchen.

"What's the matter, don't *you* trust her, either?" he asked sarcastically.

Louis frowned. "Oh, the microphones? They were installed for another purpose. A gentleman in whom we were interested kept a blonde friend in the apartment downstairs. Since the information we were trying to get was quite technical and the girl not very bright, her reports turned out to be utterly useless. . . . No," the tall man said, catching Weston's look, "Elaine wasn't here at the time, unfortunately. She is very clever about technical information. But we had to go to considerable expense to enable someone else to take down what the man said: hence the microphones."

Weston glanced again at the girl in the expensive chiffon evening gown, stirring her coffee absently with a tiny spoon. He tried to imagine her tricking and wheedling a man into talking about something he would undoubtedly know should be kept secret; getting him drunk, perhaps, teasing him, offering herself and at the last moment withholding. . . . *Elaine is very clever about technical information!* He found that he had shivered a little.

"What happened to the blonde?"

"Oh, she is on another assignment now. We retained the apartments because they were conveniently located."

Weston said, "When I called the F.B.I. this morning, they seemed to know all about this place. Doesn't that kind of limit its usefulness?"

Louis chuckled. "You'd be surprised how many places the F.B.I. know about, and we know they know about, and they know we know they know, if you follow me. It's a form of prestidigitation, fella. The hand is quicker than the eye, that kind of thing. Often we will run one kind of semi-illicit activity to distract their attention, while something entirely different and much more important is going on in the same place, unsuspected. And of course, very often they'll pursue an obvious line of inquiry to camouflage a more dangerous investigation, as you have reason to know."

"What do you mean?"

"Oh, I don't say they weren't mildly interested in questioning you yesterday, but mainly they used you as an excuse to look around the place without publicizing what they were really after."

Weston said dryly, "Is that supposed to make me feel good about it?"

"How you feel, fella," said Louis smiling, "is probably one of the least of J. Edgar Hoover's many worries."

"And what *were* they after?" Weston asked.

Louis glanced at him consideringly. "I don't suppose it's ever occurred to you," he said after a pause, "how ideal a small oil company could be for a man with, shall we say, certain outside interests. Such a company has contacts with the oil, steel, automotive, and aircraft industries, either as buyer or seller. And if the company is small enough, a man in almost any responsible job quite naturally has a knowledge of everything that's going on. He is expected to help deal with all facets of the company's business. You, yourself, as chemist, probably were in touch with most of it."

Weston nodded.

The tall man went on, "You might even have arranged to intercept various communications, apparently from customers or suppliers, if you had wanted to. Mightn't you? And then sent them on in the guise of routine correspondence? In code, of course, so that if a message went astray it would look, to the casual eye, like an ordinary business letter, or technical report, or advertisement. . . ."

"It could have been done, all right," Weston agreed calmly, while his mind grappled with the sudden question: *Who?*

Who, of the people with whom he had worked for a year and a half, had also carried a secret—better hidden than his own, which was known to both Doc and Jane

Collis? Which of them, casually offering to run down for the mail for Janie, as they all did from time to time, had been concealing behind the friendly offers a desperate urgency, had been furtively slipping the betraying, treasonable messages out of the pack on his way back upstairs. Janie herself, or even Doc . . . He realized that he was taking for granted that the thing had been worked from the laboratory, perhaps because he, himself, had become involved. But the fact that the F.B.I. had used him as an excuse did not necessarily mean they believed the guilty person to be someone close to him; his record just made him a convenient whipping boy. The letters could have been addressed to the plant foreman as bills of lading, or to Mr. French. Any of the girls in the office had access to the mail desk. *A man in almost any responsible job,* Louis had said, but you did not have to take Louis' word for it that it was a man. Anybody in the place could have done it, although for some it would have been easier than for others.

"It has been done," Louis said. "For instance, Acme has been supplying the Faircraft corporation with a rust preventive compound that hasn't been entirely satisfactory. . . ."

Weston said mechanically, "The jackasses were applying it wrong, getting too thick a coating, that's why it didn't give protection."

"Yes." Louis smiled. "There was considerable correspondence on the subject, wasn't there? You wouldn't be surprised to learn that a day or so ago a few sheets of data found their way from Faircraft to Acme that didn't concern rust preventives at all."

"I see," Weston murmured.

Louis said, "Faircraft has been running performance tests on a new jet powerplant for its army interceptor fighter. Nothing revolutionary, you understand, but very interesting. Unfortunately, the F.B.I. clamped down almost immediately the information had gone out. Our man at Faircraft was jailed. The data were traced to Acme so quickly that our agent there had no opportunity to pass them along; he had to hide them." The tall man looked up from his cup, setting it aside. "The F.B.I. were already in the place, as a matter of fact; and if you hadn't created such a fine diversion in the locker room, it's doubtful if he could have saved the situation. However, you gave him the chance he needed."

Weston had a sudden clear picture of the crowd at the locker room door, the Bentley boy holding the mail as he watched, fascinated. *One of them,* he thought, and realized that he was afraid to take it further. He did not want to find out. Two people in that group meant something special to him. He did not want to have to consider the possibility that either of them could have . . .

". . . had to give up the idea of searching the place," Louis said. "Too many pipes and kettles. So now they are, presumably, waiting for us to lead them to what they want."

"It's still there?"

"Yes. Our man has been instructed not to expose himself by making any further moves. He is a key man in this area and his position is more important to us than the papers. Even though we're interested in the Faircraft data, we'd rather lose them than jeopardize the whole organization."

"Then why doesn't he just flush the damn things down the drain?" Weston asked.

Louis smiled. "He's done better. He's taped them beneath the top right-hand drawer of your desk."

After a moment Marilyn, silent at the end of the sofa, tapped the ashes from her cigarette with the sharp nervousness with which she did almost everything these days—a little explosion of movement—then was still again. The color she had had earlier had faded from her face and the brightness from her eyes and she looked sleepy and bored. Weston looked away from her. He did not say anything. There was very little to say. The trap was self-explanatory. Louis began to explain it, anyway.

"When the papers are found, as they will be, it will look as if you'd had some motive besides bad temper for so drastically interrupting the search of your belongings. And after your past and present association with Elaine, and your having dinner with me here tonight, I don't think that one phone call to the F.B.I., or even two or three, will clear you of complicity in our operations here . . . if the papers are found." The tall man gestured to the instrument in the hall. "You're free to try it, if you want to. Call them up and tell them what you've learned. See if they thank you and get your job back for you. Personally, I think they'll guess you're double-crossing us because you've lost your nerve; or that we're throwing you overboard and you're trying to make a deal to save yourself."

"And if they settle for me, that'll leave your man free to—"

"To continue operations. That's right."

Weston said shortly, "Well, you didn't ask me up here just to crow about it. What's the proposition?"

Marilyn rose, smoothed her dress, and walked, not quite steadily, to the sideboard. Momentarily distracted, the two men watched her make herself a drink. When she did not turn around to face them, they turned back to each other.

Louis said, "Even though they're not of primary importance, we'd prefer not to lose those papers. We can't afford to risk our man to get them out, but if *you* wanted to try, there might be a little money in it for you. And of course you'd also be working in your own interests."

The tall man continued to talk, but Weston let the words go by him. The outlines of the trap were already clear in his mind: a deadfall, baited with paper and rigged to bring destruction, in the shape of the F.B.I., down on the man who reached for it. The F.B.I. would be happy to catch Paul Weston red-handed with the evidence that, incriminating enough by itself in the place where it was hidden, would be utterly damning after he had sneaked guiltily back to remove it. There was a strong probability that Louis hoped he would be caught if he tried it; Louis might even be planning to insure, by an anonymous telephone call, that this would happen.

He could leave it alone, and when the stuff was found—as he had no doubt it would be—he could try to make people believe that someone else had put it there.

He grimaced at the thought. *On me, a frame looks fine,* he reflected bitterly. Or he could, as Louis had suggested, call the F.B.I. and make like a patriot; and Louis had pointed out exactly what that would get him. It might incline them very slightly in his favor. In ten years perhaps, if he behaved himself properly, they might check back over the records and decide that Weston, Paul F., hadn't been such a bad guy after all, and it was a pity the poor sap had died of starvation, but some mistakes were inevitable and the country's safety had been preserved.

He heard his own voice. "Tonight?"

Louis said, "I'll meet you in the park with the money, afterward. Do you know the parking lot down by the lakefront—?" He described the place carefully. It sounded, Weston thought, like a particularly good place for a murder.

V

There was a fine mist of rain in the air as he drove up the narrow street toward the familiar building. The street lights had haloes that looked cottony, like the stuff you blow off dandelion stems in the spring. From a distance he could see the small parking lot squeezed between the plant and the next factory—which bottled some kind of soft drink—empty except for the watchman's rusty sedan parked close to the side door. He drew up his own car, not much younger, behind it, turned out the lights and got out.

Presently he turned up the convertible collar of his gabardine topcoat and buttoned it to the throat. The dinner jacket beneath it made him feel uncomfortable and out of place. Somebody was undoubtedly watching him, he thought, and to hell with them. The side door was locked when he tried it. He shook it, and kicked it tentatively. The noise seemed to roll out across the empty parking lot, echoing and re-echoing among the silent factories around, before it died away.

They could hear him, he thought, clear up to the Loop. Somewhere, distantly, a streetcar went by, but no cars came down the near-by street. He was apparently the only person in the neighborhood; yet somewhere, he was certain, there were men watching him. Even if the plant itself were not being watched—which seemed unlikely if there were any truth in Louis's story—Weston was sure that at least one person had been following him. He was probably leading a parade around the streets of Chicago. *Me and the Pied Piper,* he thought.

He had made no effort to give them the slip, for the simple reason that he had no idea of how to go about it, and his old car would not do much over forty, anyway. Similarly, he had given up any thought of getting into the building unobserved. If men were watching the place they were sure to be better at this cops-and-robbers routine than he was. One thing you learned in scientific work was never to challenge a specialist in his own field, if you could help it. *Keep it simple,* he thought, *have a straight story to tell if they stop you. Whether they believe it or not doesn't matter. They don't believe anything you tell them, anyway.* If anybody stopped him, he would merely have decided, a little intoxicated, that tonight was a good time to clean out his desk and locker.

He shook the door again. The watchman was probably asleep in the boiler room where it was warm and dry; or he was doing his rounds, grumbling, among the big storage tanks along the spur railroad track that serviced the plant. Weston swore loudly and walked around the corner of the building, made his way through the stacked oil drums waiting to be cleaned at the rear of the plant and along the track to the big sliding doors at which the cars were loaded and unloaded. He threw his weight against the small trap-door in one of them, pushing down, and after a moment the latch slipped free. This was no secret to anybody who worked in the place with the possible exception of Mr. French.

Weston left the trap-door open behind him so that

nobody could claim he was trying to hide his presence in the place. Ahead of him in the long, low room he could make out the shapes of the silent mixing vats and the rows on rows of drums—some empty, clean, and waiting to be filled; others full and waiting to be emptied. The only light was a naked sixty-watt bulb hanging in front of the foreman's office by the fire doors at the far end, closed for the night. He started toward it and stopped abruptly, listening to a rat run across the floor upstairs. You could tell when it left the wooden floor and started scrabbling across the tops of the steel drums stored up there. Weston grimaced in the semi-darkness, annoyed with himself for the way his heart had pounded. *They'll never make a hero of you, bud,* he told himself, and made his way to the light, where he paused to scrape caked grease off his shoes. *Or even much of a villain,* he thought, finding himself casting uneasy looks into the shadows among the surrounding oil drums. He had been on night-shift several times when they were putting out a big order, but somehow it was different, being alone in the place. *Who says you're alone?* he asked himself, wincing as two rats took off in different directions over his head.

A small steel door beside the closed fire doors let him into the shipping room beyond; and then he was climbing the stairs past the main office. The glass partitions let him see the unmanned switchboard and deserted desks. As was customary at night, the door to Mr. French's office had been left open, with a fluorescent lamp casting a cold light over the desk in there, and no other light in the room.

Upstairs, the door to Dr. Lowery's office was closed and locked. This was not customary and made him uneasy. Well, if they were waiting in there for him, there was nothing he could do about it, he decided, and looked around the laboratory, seeing the reagent bottles in neat rows above the stone-topped tables, the apparatus and glassware gleaming faintly in the light of the single ceiling fixture left burning. Finally he let his glance go to the group of desks in the far corner, beyond the somewhat larger desk—equipped with a typewriter—that belonged to Jane Collis.

The question he had put aside came back to cry for an answer: *Who?* The occupants of those desks were clearly the people best located for planting something in his desk. . . . *You'd better make sure the stuff's there before you start theorizing about it,* he reminded himself sharply. But it took a moment, and an effort, before he could make himself go forward. He felt that sirens would scream and bells start ringing when he touched the second desk from the right; the doors would fill with armed men and, caught with the evidence in his hands, he would be dragged away to be tried as a spy with the verdict a foregone conclusion. *What the hell,* he thought, *in jail they've got to feed me. . . .*

The drawer made a small rumbling sound as he pulled it out. There was nothing beneath it.

Quickly, he checked all the other drawers, finding that for the first time he was really frightened. It was to have been expected that Louis had lied, but he found that he had not expected the lie to have no basis in fact at all. . . . He pulled the top right-hand drawer out completely and turned it over to the light. Four small tabs of transparent tape made a rectangle on the plywood bottom; a corner of a sheet of paper adhered to one. It was too small to give a clue to what the paper had been, but there clearly had been something there. Somebody had merely got here ahead of him.

When the door opened behind him he found that he was ready for it, waiting for it. He did not turn at once, giving the person behind him plenty of time for whatever he wanted to do. If he was to be shot, it was no break to see it coming; and if the F.B.I. were there he did not want to startle them into doing anything hasty. After seeing him blow his top once they would be understandably careful not to take chances with him a second time. A voice spoke his name softly, calling him Wes.

"Hello, Janie," he said. His mouth was dry and he did not like to think what her presence meant.

She was standing in the doorway to Dr. Lowery's

office, now open. There was a gun in her hand. She had on one of those long, loose, hooded coats that the girls had been wearing the past year or so; this one was brown and he knew it as well as the clothes in his own wardrobe, having carried it for her and helped her into it innumerable times. He knew the low shoes she was wearing, and the shell-rimmed glasses—one of two pairs she owned—and the way she had her dark hair drawn back into a bun at the nape of her neck. But he did not know the pinched white face, or the wide, intent eyes behind the thick-lensed glasses.

He said, "Are you going to shoot me, Janie?" His mind started to add it all up. He did not like the answer he reached, or really believe it. Yet who had been better situated to intercept incoming mail, who had had more constant access to his desk than the small girl in front of him?

"You," she said. "I . . . thought . . ."

"What?"

"I thought you didn't . . . didn't . . ."

"Didn't what?"

"Know," she said.

He looked at her, never letting himself look away from her, not for a moment. "It isn't there," he said.

"No," she said. "I've got it." The fingers of her left hand crushed the pocket of her coat from the outside, crumpling paper beneath the cloth.

"You weren't supposed to," he said.

She stared at him blankly.

He asked quietly, "Why did you come here?"

"I thought you—" Her face seemed to go through a spasm of pain. "I thought you—"

"What?" He was getting closer, slowly. The palms of his hands were wet, and he could feel the perspiration inside the starched collar of his shirt. "What did you think, Janie?"

"I thought you didn't know. . . ." She looked up at him. The gun sagged, forgotten, in her hand. "This morning . . . Doc asked me for your notebook. Something—paper—caught when I tried to close the drawer. I thought

. . . I told myself you didn't know . . . Somebody else . . . I came back to . . ." The gun steadied and her knuckles whitened. "But you did know. You went right to it. I watched you." She stared at him blindly. He saw that she was crying.

She turned and leaned her forehead against the doorjamb, and did not seem to know when he took the gun away. He stood for a moment beside her, sickeningly relieved to have his hands on the weapon, so that for a moment nothing else mattered. The small girl in the brown coat pressed her face hard against the unyielding wood of the door and continued to cry silently.

"No," she gasped, when he tried to take her by the shoulders, "no, don't touch me. At least don't touch me!"

He looked at the gun in his hand. "Janie, the gun," he said. "Where'd you get the gun?"

"He had it," she said, and made a little motion with her head toward the office. Weston looked at the familiar desk where, as on Mr. French's desk downstairs, a small lamp was burning to give all the light there was in the room except for what spilled in through the open door. At the base of the desk he saw the head and one shoulder of the man who was lying on the rug behind it, unmistakably dead.

VI

He was thinking that this did not happen, even as he walked deliberately forward and checked that he had made no error either about the identity or the condition of the man on the floor: it was Dr. Lowery and he was dead. Weston looked down at the silent figure, seeing the drying blood on the vest and on the fingers of the hand that must have gone there in an instinctive movement to contain the sudden unbearable pain, even as death wiped this out with everything else the older man had ever known. Doc, he thought, who had hired him even knowing how he had come to lose his previous job; Doc, with his air of a somewhat uneasy champion of the oppressed and misunderstood, who would gladly have tackled Mr. French in his behalf. Or would he really? Doc, to whom the laboratory mail came quite naturally, without any effort on his part. Doc, who had an unquestioned right to be anywhere in the building he wanted to be, who could openly look through anybody's desk on the excuse—if anybody asked, which they wouldn't, except to help—of hunting for a scrap of data or some mislaid correspondence. . . .

Weston turned to look at the small girl in the doorway. The light was brighter in the laboratory behind her than in the dim office in which he stood, so that it was hard for him to see her face. After a while, she nodded dumbly in answer to his unspoken question. *Yes,* the gesture said, *I killed him.*

This did not happen, Weston thought: people you knew did not shoot other people you knew. They could have peculiar politics, be engaged in questionable activities, but they did not kill each other.

"Why?" he asked.

"I . . . he . . ."

It was too much for her, and she turned away. Weston looked at the dead man on the floor and tried to work it out by himself; but a small urgent voice was speaking in his mind: *Wake up, bud, you haven't got all night.*

He came out of the office, closing the door behind him after setting the latch so that it would not lock. For a moment he was under the impression that she must have run away, and found himself curiously relieved not to have to decide what to do or believe about her. But she was leaning against the wall at his shoulder, her back to the wall, her hands flat against it, as if she needed all the contact she could get with something solid. He stood looking down at her.

Once, he remembered, he had given this girl a ring which she still had around somewhere, and had planned to marry her. It seemed remote and distant now; and he knew that he had been reaching for matrimony only as a rung in the ladder back up to the security and respectability that had been taken from him by what had happened in Washington. The knowledge made him feel uncomfortable in front of her, so that when he spoke his voice was rougher than he had intended.

"Give," he said.

She seemed about to protest; then she pulled a crumpled envelope from her pocket and held it out to him. It was addressed to the Chemical Laboratory, Acme Petroleum Corporation, and it had been opened. He drew out the contents, two sheets that at first glance seemed to be laboratory report forms of a type sometimes used at Acme, each filled out for some oil. A hasty check of the physical characteristics showed him that they were inconsistent and meaningless. No such petroleum compounds had ever, to his knowledge, been discovered; nor did he think any were ever likely to be. Code, Louis had said. Weston returned the papers to the envelope.

"You came back for this, Janie?"

She did not look at him. "Yes."

"Why? What were you going to do with it?"

"Give it to you," she whispered.

He did not want to believe her, because it would put him so deeply in her debt. *Hold on,* he told himself, *look this over carefully, bud, before you buy it. You were a sucker for a girl once before, remember.*

"Go on."

"When I felt it under the drawer . . ." She looked rigidly at the floor. "It obviously didn't belong there . . . I thought somebody else must have . . . I was afraid those men would find it and think you . . . I thought if you saw it you might be able to . . ."

Her glance slid up to touch his face, and down again. He could see her bitterly remembering seeing him walk straight across the laboratory to examine the drawer in question. There was no reason why she should believe an explanation, so he did not make one.

He asked, "How'd you get back in, Janie?"

"I never left," she whispered. "I just went outside at

47

five to make it look as if . . . and then I slipped back in and hid in the washroom."

"You've been here since five o'clock!" He glanced at his watch, which read well after ten. Janie nodded. He asked, "What made you think somebody was watching?"

"Well, I thought—" she flushed "—I thought that if it was a movie, they would be. And then, while I was looking out the window, I saw him. He was in the doorway across the street for a while, then he moved into the alley beside that window-shade factory. So I knew I'd have to wait until dark to get out without being seen. I got myself something to eat and drink from the vending machines in the plant, and went back into the washroom to wait. The watchman looked in once, but he didn't come inside. After a while I went up and . . . and got it." She glanced at the letter in his hand. "It was getting dark, it was about eight, and I thought I could make it out through the back if I went through the drum-cleaning shed and got in among the storage tanks. Only, when I started to leave, *he* was there." She did not quite look at the closed door beside her. "He said he'd seen me sneak back. He said he'd been waiting to see what I . . . was up to."

"And then?"

"He—" She closed her hands into fists; it was not a gesture of anger, but of remembered panic. "He wasn't the same person at all, Wes! He had a gun and he made me go into his office and he closed the door and called up somebody he called Louis. . . ." She looked up and spoke with careful clarity: "He wanted to know when Louis was going to send *you*. . . ."

"Me?" Weston asked, surprised although it was logical enough when he thought about it. When you had two people to get rid of—and doubtless something drastic had been planned for him earlier, for which Janie's interference had made her also a candidate—it was easier to take care of them both at once.

Janie looked away and said stiffly, "Louis was to see that somebody named Weston came here as soon as possible." She waited, as if hoping he would have something to say.

"I—" He checked himself; there was no time for explanations. "Go on, Janie."

"Then we waited for you. The watchman came up the stairs once, but *he* took me into the private washroom back of the office, and the man didn't look there." She drew a long breath. "Then we waited some more. Then he suddenly remembered the envelope and had me bring it to him. He was sitting at the desk. I guess it was so . . . *so usual,* my bringing him a letter to read, that he forgot . . . He started to read and the gun was just lying there beside him. When I leaned over and picked it up his face got so surprised, and he reached for it and . . . and it shot him." She licked her lips. "I mean, I shot him. I suppose I did."

He wanted to help her but he did not dare to touch her. After a while he asked, "How long ago was this?"

"I don't know," she said. "How could I know? It seemed like ages before I heard you. . . . I was so afraid the watchman would come by and wonder why the door was locked."

Weston frowned, trying to follow her reasoning. "You waited for me, even after what you'd heard him—"

"I guess I just wanted to be sure," she said, and looked up at him with sudden, disconcerting steadiness. Presently she said quietly, "I guess I've been kind of a little fool, haven't I, Wes?"

He found himself unable to meet her eyes. He wanted to explain himself, but was stopped by the cold fact that would not be explained: that he had nothing to give her in return for the feeling she must have had for him, to try to do this for him. There was only one thing he could do, and he thought: *make it good now; get her out of here.* Her question showed him the way.

He said carefully, clearing his throat, "Well, I wouldn't say *that,* Janie."

Slowly the color came flooding into her face; she had obviously been waiting for him to reassure her, to assert his innocence and his love for her. Whether or not she had intended to let him convince her, she had been waiting for him to try.

He said angrily, "Don't look at me like that, Janie. When you spend four years of your life in uniform and all it gets you is a ten-point veteran's preference toward a lousy civil service job, which they then grab away from you because they don't like your female companions, what are you supposed to do, get up and sing 'The Star-Spangled Banner'?"

She licked her dry lips. "I wasn't thinking about that," she whispered. He realized that she was afraid of him. He was somebody, now, that she did not know; and she would not have been surprised to see him take out the gun and try to kill her.

He said, "I'm not going to shoot you, Janie, you can let go of that wall!" He waited until she had straightened up. Then he jerked his head toward the closed door. "He killed himself. You weren't here. You went to see the show at the Park Theater—we saw the feature downtown last week, but you didn't realize that until you'd got inside, and you didn't care about the picture, anyway; you were just worrying about me." He saw her wince, and went on: "Then you went home to bed. You can't help it if they lost track of you; nobody'd told you to keep yourself available. If they ask how you got home from here, you took a streetcar. If nobody saw you, that isn't your fault."

She shook her head in weak protest. "But I *can't* just—"

He said irritably, "Don't let your conscience get the better of you. If they get the wrong person you can always stand up and say you did it, can't you?"

"Why are you—"

"Look," he said, "don't ask so many questions. I'm giving you a break, Janie. Because you're a nice girl. You don't want to get mixed up in this."

"You might . . . have thought of that sooner," she breathed.

He said, "Damn it, I didn't ask you to go around killing people for me."

"No," she whispered, "no, you just gave me a ring and said you loved me." She never stopped watching him. "Wes, why are you helping me now? What do you want now?"

After a moment he made himself grin. "All right," he said. "All right, Janie." He slapped the letter against the palm of his hand. "This," he said, "this never existed. As long as this never existed, you never shot anybody. Do you understand, Janie? Letter, murder. No letter, no murder. . . ."

"It wasn't mur—"

"Do you think anybody's going to believe that, Janie? When you tell them why you came back here, they'll think you were my accomplice right along; you just got caught slipping this letter out of here for me, and killed him. Why, that's just about what happened, isn't it? How are you going to prove what your motives were; and who's going to care?"

Her glance touched the rectangle of paper, and returned to his face. Her own face looked drained and exhausted, as if she had been through a long illness. "I shouldn't let you . . ." she whispered. "Oh, I don't know what's *right* any more!"

Her voice said that she knew only too well what was right; and then her shoulders sagged a little, in surrender. She pulled at the buttons of her coat and reached inside. Her hand came out with a small object threaded on a string about her neck. She pulled hard, the string broke, and she dropped the thing into his hand and, whirling, ran for the stairs.

Presently Weston looked down at the engagement ring gleaming, with all the gleam you could buy for sixty-nine fifty these days, in the palm of his hand. He dropped it into his trousers pocket. He found that he was a little disappointed in Jane Collis. She should have marched bravely out to tell the F.B.I. all about the letter, even if it meant the electric chair. Perhaps she was going to do it after all, but remembering her small, weary face, he doubted it. Not tonight. And the longer she let it ride, the harder it would come. *So long, Janie.*

After a long time, hearing nothing to indicate that she had not got clear all right, he opened the office door and went in to the dead man, with the feeling of disturbing somebody's privacy. He took the gun from his pocket and studied it from all angles against the light. It was a small revolver and he was not surprised that the sound of it had not been heard outside this third-floor office insulated for air conditioning. Only a couple of fingerprints seemed clear enough to be of any use to anybody. He smeared these lightly and put the gun on the rug, not too far from the body.

Straightening up, he looked around the place and thought of a dozen things he could do to make the scene more convincing. *Don't get fancy now,* he warned himself, *come along, Mastermind, before you louse it up.* All that was necessary was to leave the possibility of suicide open. He went out of the office, releasing the catch so that the door locked irretrievably behind him: he intended to claim that it had been locked when he came and that he had therefore never looked inside. Then he took the papers from his pocket and studied them grimly.

It seemed to him a little anticlimactic to discover that they were really no problem at all. He walked to one of the fume-hoods and pulled the switch beside it; an exhaust fan set up a muted roaring in the metal duct that led outdoors. He burned the papers in the largest crucible the lab provided, and used a Bunsen burner to complete the job of incineration. Faircraft presumably had the data on tap, and nobody else had any real business with them, anyway. Finished, he felt rather noble and patriotic—he could, after all, have got a considerable amount of money for them, assuming he could have got them away from here—but the temptation had really not been very strong. Apparently, you either had to be born a traitor or get extremely hungry; and he was not yet that hungry.

VII

They let him get three blocks before they stopped him. Weston had never been searched before, and the experience left him angry and humiliated. Only the memory of what was behind him in the locked third-floor office enabled him to keep his temper under control. He watched them go through the carton of personal belongings which he had, when leaving the place, put into the rear seat without any attempt at concealment, and through the car itself. Finally the big man, whose bandaged wrist gave him a reason for liking Weston no better than Weston liked him, came back along the sidewalk.

"You picked a funny time to drop by for your stuff."

Weston said, "Maybe we just don't agree on what's funny."

Richardson studied him thoughtfully. "You called me this morning. You offered to help us." After a moment he went on: "It may interest you to know that we got an anonymous telephone call telling us you'd try to break in here tonight. We were giving you a chance to bring it out to us. . . ."

"What?" Weston asked.

"What you were sent here to get."

Weston said, "What I came after is in the back seat."

The big man looked him over coldly. "You're getting by with a lot of stuff, Mac," he murmured, and shifted the position of his injured arm as a reminder. "We're leaning over backward to go easy on you, because we think you *may* have got a raw deal. But don't push your credit too far."

Weston waited, unimpressed. When the other remained silent, he asked, "May I go now?"

The big man hesitated, clearly quite aware that there was trickery involved here, and debating the best way to handle it: whether to let Weston go for now, or take him back to Acme and hold him while an attempt was made to discover what he had been doing in the place. It seemed to Weston that midnight passed and dawn approached while he waited for the answer. He knew that he was not a good enough actor to behave naturally while waiting for them to discover Dr. Lowery's body. They would know he had known it was there.

"I guess you can run along, for now," the big man said reluctantly.

Weston turned toward his car without, he hoped, any appearance of haste.

"Oh, Weston . . ."

This was part of the technique, he knew: to make you think you were safe, and then slug you unexpectedly from behind. He straightened up. *Don't talk too much, now!* he warned himself.

"Yes?"

"Where's your girl friend?"

"Marilyn?" he asked, making his voice surprised. "She was at the apartment when I left."

The big man chuckled. "You and your women! No, the little girl. She seems to've given our man the slip; we really haven't got enough people to keep an eye on everybody."

Weston said, "Well, good for Janie. I didn't think she had it in her." He hoped his voice indicated that Janie's whereabouts did not interest him enough to speculate about them.

"I noticed," Richardson murmured, "that she seems to've given you back your ring. Or do you always carry a spare engagement ring in your pocket?"

It was like seeing an open manhole in the road ahead when you were doing seventy; for a moment he could not seem to catch his breath, until he realized that the other could not readily know that the ring had been returned tonight.

He heard his own voice saying smoothly, "No, she gave it back, all right. What did you expect after the reputation you've given me?" When the big man did not speak at once he went on to ask with innocent curiosity, "How did you know we were engaged?"

"Everybody in the place seemed to know about it. Was it supposed to be a secret?"

"Kind of," Weston said and, knowing that he had said enough on the subject, waited, feeling the ring heavy and betraying in his pocket. He had not even thought about it; and Richardson had not given a sign that he had noticed it, until now. It occurred to Weston that he had underestimated the man he was trying to outwit. The thought was not reassuring.

The F.B.I. man said deliberately, "Well, I guess you can go. . . . Oh, just one thing more."

Weston waited by the car without speaking.

"It was a woman who called us," the big man said. "Nice sexy voice."

"Thanks."

"You haven't been a sucker for that one again, have you?"

"What do I do, say yes?"

Richardson laughed. As Weston bent to get into the car, he asked quietly, "Oh . . . you haven't seen your friend Dr. Lowery tonight, have you?"

Weston felt his breathing stop, his heart stop. It seemed to him that the picture in his mind, of the dead man lying on the rug in the blue-white light of the fluorescent desk lamp, must be visible to everyone around him.

He glanced over his shoulder. "You seem to have a hell of a time keeping track of people," he said. "What do you want Doc for?"

The big man regarded him without liking. "Never mind," he said. "Beat it. . . ."

It was raining a little when Weston left the car near the tall apartment buildings that faced the park, and went inside the closest one. He did not really know why he had come back here, except that there was no other place to go except his room, and he needed to talk to someone. The buzzer responded to his finger on the proper button without any questions from the voice-box. Marilyn was waiting for him at the apartment door when he got out of the elevator. He did not think she had been expecting him. She stepped back to let him in, however, and he stopped to look at her for a brief moment as he passed her, a little shocked to see how slender and lovely and serene she looked, facing him. Somehow it would have been nicer to find her disheveled and reeling drunk. It was not pleasant to know that people could look as she looked and still be what she was.

He walked directly across the living room to the sideboard and poured himself a powerful drink. Then, on consideration, he returned half the slug to the bottle; his trained chemist's hand performing the task without spilling a drop. That was all the training was good for now, mixing drinks, he reflected bitterly. But it was clearly no time to be getting tight.

With the glass in his hand he turned again to look at her. She had not followed him across the room, but was standing by the little hallway, watching him. Something in her regard reminded him that he still had his hat on and was therefore no gentleman.

"I thought you were going to meet Louis in the park," she said.

"Uhuh."

"Have you seen him?"

"No."

"Did you have . . . any trouble?" The small break betrayed her utterly.

"Should I have had?" he asked, and watched her turn and go to the windows, the short chiffon gown she still wore swirling and eddying about her like mist. After a while, he said, "You're kind of a bitch, aren't you, Lynn?"

"I suppose so." She did not move or look at him.

"Whose idea was it, yours or his?"

"His."

"You'd say so, of course."

"Yes."

"But *you* called the F.B.I."

"Yes."

"The man said you had a nice sexy voice."

"Did he?"

"I was to be caught with the goods on me?"

"Yes."

"You'll be disappointed to hear it didn't work," he said. "Because I burned the stuff."

She turned then. The motion continued in her dress for a little after she was still again. He finished his drink, set the glass aside carefully, and walked across the room to her. She waited for him to reach her, unmoving. She did not seem to be afraid.

"You lousy little tramp," he said, standing over her. "I ought to beat your ears down."

"Yes," she said.

He pulled her to him roughly, to maul her, rumple her, to muss her fragile gown and her careful dignity, to hurt and humble her. But somehow the kiss did not turn out like that at all; and after a while he released her abruptly, bewildered and a little frightened by what had happened to his angry intentions. He found himself irrelevantly remembering that she had stepped behind him at a certain moment earlier this evening, probably to help disarm him, yet just possibly to shield him.

"What the hell are you, anyway?" he asked.

She turned away from him to look down at the headlights passing along the drives of the park across the street. The pavements were shiny with wetness. He stood behind her for a while, waiting for her to speak, until he realized from her breathing that she was trying very hard to keep from crying. Then he started to turn away, but she heard him move and stopped him with her hand.

"Don't—"

"What?"

"I thought you were leaving."

He shook his head. "Just shedding my hat and coat. Okay with you?"

She smiled at his challenging tone. Her voice was suddenly quite prosaic. "Bring me my evening bag from the telephone stand, will you? I need a hanky, for some reason."

In the hallway, he glanced at his watch; twenty minutes had passed now since the F.B.I. had let him drive away. They would be in the Acme building now, they would be up in the laboratory; if they had managed to locate the watchman with the key, they might already have the office open. Once Dr. Lowery was found, they would be after Paul Weston again. He had no doubt that somebody was keeping track of him; it should not take them long to get here. Anticipation of the questions they would ask this time made him cringe inwardly, and he wondered if he would be able to stick to the story that the door had been locked and he had not known what lay behind it. Even so, he thought there was a very good chance that he would wind up being tried for murder. Well, you could not say he had not asked for it.

When you came right down to it, he reflected, you would have to go a long way to find another man who went to more trouble to play sucker for every woman who crossed his path. *And the wenches aren't even grateful!* he thought, remembering Janie's small, hostile, shamed face as she gave him back his ring and fled. Well, what did he want, he asked himself, a tin medal on a pink ribbon? She had gone, hadn't she? The trouble was, nobody seemed to appreciate what an innately fine and heroic person Paul Weston really was. *Pass the crying towel this way.*

He wondered if Janie would speak up if he were arrested. Once he would have had no doubts, but now he was not so sure. Thinking him to be a spy, a man who had used her and perhaps even laughed at her, Janie might very well let him be punished for what she had done, feeling that it was really his fault anyway, and that it would serve him right. And if she did not come forward of her own accord, he would only make himself look like a coward and a vicious fool if he tried to save himself by bringing her into it. Even if she were to volunteer a confession, there was a strong probability it would be thought that, still in love with him, she was lying to protect him. No, the story was his and he was stuck with it; in this game, apparently, you played for keeps.

When he came back into the living room, Marilyn was sitting at the end of the long sofa nursing an unlighted cigarette, which she held up to him for a match. Somehow it was a relief to be with someone to whom he owed nothing, someone who could not be harmed by knowing him, because she was already infected with the contagion it seemed he carried. In fact, when you came right down to it, it was she who had given it to him.

"Thanks," she said, leaning back from the flame he had held for her. "What happened to my purse?"

He laughed. "Sorry. I was thinking about something else. Shall I—?"

She shook her head. "Do you want another drink?" she asked.

"No," he said. "Do you?"

"No," she murmured. "Even if I *am* a lush who's been tanking up all day, Paul, I don't want a drink, thank you."

He winced to hear the words he had spoken upstairs quoted back at him: they sounded crude and unpleasant.

She said, "You don't have to make me out worse than I am."

"I'm sorry."

Remembering the microphones in this apartment, he did not try to explain. He was not very eager, anyway, to confess that he had still retained enough illusions about her to think she might have been trying to help him, that he had, by reviling her, been trying to shield her from the suspicion of her associates.

After a while he seated himself on the sofa beside her. Presently she put her hand on his arm lightly, as if to call his attention to what she was about to tell him.

"I did try to keep you from being involved in Washington, Paul," she said. "Even if you don't believe it. And I warned you this morning to get out. If you keep playing Secret Agent X-9 around the place, is it my fault if you get into trouble? Certainly I called the F.B.I.; I'd have done it even if Louis hadn't told me to, just to get you put out of circulation for a while."

"Why?" he asked.

She watched the ascending spiral of smoke from her cigarette. "If you saw a little kid loose in your laboratory, reaching for stuff that could burn him or kill him——" She looked at him with sudden directness. "And do you think I like having you around with that hangdog look, blaming me for everything that's happened to you since the day you were born, Paul? Do you think I like being needled and insulted and sneered at, yes, even struck——" she touched her cheek where a small bruise was still visible, "——just so you can keep on telling yourself you're not still in love with me? I'm not much to be in love with, I admit, but have I ever done anything to take advantage of the fact that you go all rubber-legged when I kiss you? Have I? In Washington, did I ever ask you for anything, anything at all? As I remember, I was even very careful to go easy on your pocketbook when we went out together. Here, have I used my . . . my sex on you to make you do anything but get the hell out of something you don't know anything about and haven't the experience to handle? Or, if you're going to be stubborn and get your fool head shot off, to treat me with ordinary human decency until it happens? I haven't, have I?"

"No," he said stiffly.

"All right," she said. "And another thing, I don't like to be looked at and handled as if I were some kind of a tart, Paul. I'm not. Maybe it's nothing to my credit that I don't operate in the bedroom like the girl who had this place before me, but it just happens that I don't. That's just another conclusion you've jumped to——"

"I never said——"

She said, rather breathlessly, "You've been waiting for me to start seducing you ever since I picked you up last night! Well, if you stay here tonight, you'll still sleep on this couch, Paul. In Washington, I was a messenger, nothing more. I had dates with those men and afterward there would be something in my purse and then I'd go somewhere else and there wouldn't be anything in my purse any longer. I'm not claiming that's anything to be proud of; and I'm not saying that at twenty-five I'm as innocent as I was at fifteen; but that's my private life and my own business, and you can just keep wondering about it from now until you grow a long gray beard. But the next time you start to push me around, darling, I'm not going to be sweet and girlish and yielding: I'm going to crown you with a lamp. It isn't as if you were used to acting that way. It isn't as if you'd dream of acting that way with any other girl you know. Well, you're not going to act that way with me, either, Paul."

He did not speak. She got up and stabbed her cigarette into an ashtray, which was already half full of stubs she must have put there, waiting, while he was at Acme. The trays had all been empty, earlier that evening. She turned to look at him.

"You've got no right—" she began quickly.

"No right to what?"

"—to condemn. . . . Oh, I guess you have," she whispered. "I suppose you can't divide a person up into different parts and judge them all separately, can you? The funny thing is that quite often I still feel like quite a nice person, Paul, and when somebody like you treats me as if I were . . . rubbish . . . it hurts. Of course you know that. That's why you do it, isn't it?"

He asked, "How did you get into this racket, anyway?"

"It wasn't a racket when I got into it," she said after a little pause. "It was more like a religion. You can do a lot of strange things for something you believe in; things that seem quite incomprehensible after you've stopped. You just can't see how you could have been so blind. . . . But of course, it was very breathless and thrilling, too; and that had something to do with it. I used to like excitement," she said, rather dryly.

He did not speak. Presently she came back to the sofa and sat down on the edge of it, facing him. "I don't suppose you'd ever understand," she said quietly. "I've never tried to make anybody . . . It really was like a religion. I was a nice girl from a wealthy family—they don't know where I am now or what name I'm using—and they used to have fits about the political views I came home with. They couldn't see where I got them. But . . . it just seemed like the answer, when I was in college.

The world we lived in had come all apart during the depression, but nobody at home would admit there was anything wrong with it, or that anything should be done about it. The self-righteous way they talked because *we* could afford . . . The way they closed their eyes to *everything*. . . . And then a boy gave me a book to read, and I went with him to a meeting—I don't even remember his name, now—and it was like coming into a different place, where nobody was afraid to believe, really believe, that the world could be made into a wonderful place to live in, if you were just willing to work and suffer for it."

Her face had seemed to soften and become young and almost eager as she talked. "And what they believed in," she said, "had a sort of beautiful, simple logic, and if it was harsh and cruel in a way, what's a revolution when you're seventeen years old? What are a few hundred thousand people to be murdered in cold blood, when you're a sophomore in college and haven't ever seen anybody dead? And if you really couldn't stomach the revolution, there were always people who'd help you argue it wouldn't be necessary. Why, it was the official line: nothing violent, nothing illegal. We believed it, why shouldn't we? We believed everything they told us!" Her features were sharp now with self-contempt; and she looked at least thirty years old. "What nobody, *nobody* seems to realize is that we *weren't* betraying our country. We thought we were helping to save it. Along with the rest of the world."

"And now?" he asked gently.

"Now we're all running to the nearest platform to wash our dirty little disillusionments in public." She shivered. "But for some of us it's too late. We've already done too much. . . . Did you know that a man in Washington killed himself two years ago because of something he'd passed along to me? He was about to be discovered, so he killed himself."

Weston shook his head; he had not heard it.

She said, "They hushed it up. He was in the State Department. He left a note. That's why I had to disappear like that. *Now* do you see why I can't . . . why I have to keep on . . . ?" She rose again, standing with her back to him. "I suppose if I were really brave . . . but I'm not. And *they* know it. They always know just what kind of person you are, and what you can be made to do, and how to make you do it. They know that as long as I can keep on living in nice places and wearing nice clothes and having people admire me, I'm not going to help put myself in jail if I can avoid it. They don't worry because I no longer think I'm saving the world . . . you won't believe it, Paul, but I really thought that in Washington— as late as that, two years ago!—I was working for world peace. Until I learned what some of the documents were I'd helped pass along, and where they'd gone to; and until the foreign situation made it so obvious what was going on over there that even I began to understand. . . ." She turned to look down at him. "I'm not asking you to feel sorry for me, darling. Why, a lot of the time I still kind of enjoy myself, in a ham-actressy sort of way. It's, well, *exciting*—" She shivered again, and after a pause walked away across the room, saying, "I think I will have a drink after all. Join me?"

"All right," he said. "Just a little one."

As he went forward to take it from her, he did not know what he was thinking, except that it was tinged with regret. Because it was too late to be explaining anything. It was too late. Even if he were in love with her, it was too late for love. He would wind up in court for murder, and she for something many people would consider worse than murder; and how they had got that way no longer really mattered.

Yet it was nice to have company. He smiled at her, taking the glass from her hand, and her smile answered him; then suddenly died. He also had heard the elevator come to a stop at this floor; but he stared at her for a moment longer, and understood that she, too, had been waiting. She, too, was expecting someone or something. She had been a little surprised to see him, he remembered suddenly, she had thought herself to be opening the door for somebody else; someone for whom she had, he reminded himself, retained the fragile, becoming evening gown instead of changing into something more comfortable and less vulnerable.

Her glance at him was suddenly the glance of a stranger, as she put her glass aside and went hastily toward the door, but not so quickly that the bell did not have time to ring before she got there.

Then Louis was in the hallway. Weston heard the tall man's voice.

"Where?"

Marilyn answered with a jerk of her head. Louis brushed past her to stand in the archway, facing Weston. Behind him, the slender fair-haired girl Weston could no longer feel he knew had turned aside to pick up her silver-mesh evening bag from the telephone stand. She did not look around.

"What took you so long?" she asked sullenly of the tall man. "God, I've had to tell him the whole story of my life, waiting for you to get here!"

"I know," Louis said. "I heard you."

The girl behind him glanced up quickly at the tone of his voice.

VIII

Louis was wearing an army officer's bulky trenchcoat; his hand was in the pocket of the coat. The garment became him, giving him an air of reckless arrogance that was not belied by his handsome bared head. Yet somehow with a gun in his hand he was not quite as impressive a figure as without one, talking about it: he had a little of the appearance of a man running a bluff and not quite sure it was going over.

"Where's his hat and coat?"

Marilyn, after a moment, straightened up and slipped her wrist into the loop of the silver purse with which she had been toying.

"I'll get them."

She crossed to the closet, then carried the clothes through the living room to Weston, taking a route that did not at any time place her between the two men. She gave Weston the coat to put on, waited until he had buttoned it, and then presented him with the hat.

Louis said, "Take a look down the fire escape, will you, Elaine?"

"What's the matter with the elevator?"

"Nothing. Just an agent of the F.B.I. making sure your friend doesn't get away before the police can arrest him for murder. . . . The fire escape!" he prompted sharply, as Marilyn made as if to speak. "We haven't got all night."

She glanced at Weston a little strangely before turning away. Weston obeyed the tall man's signal and followed her. As he entered the kitchen, she was coming back in through the open fire escape door.

"It seems all clear," she said to Louis.

"All right," he said deliberately. "You go first, Elaine."

Her head came up. "But *I'm* not—" She checked herself, watching him. "But why, Louis?"

The tall man said nothing. She shrugged her bare shoulders resignedly.

"Well, I suppose it's all right if I get myself a wrap," she said.

As she turned to slip past them sideways—the two men leaving only a small space for her in the tiny kitchen— Louis moved without warning and pinned her with hip and shoulder against the refrigerator while still facing Weston, who heard her quick gasp of shock and surprise at the unexpected roughness. It took the tall man an instant to jerk the silver-mesh bag from her wrist. He stepped back again, in releasing her throwing her away from him toward the open door, where the raised step tripped her.

Louis dropped the captured purse on the drainboard, pried the throat of it open left-handed, caught hold of something inside, and shook it free. The discarded purse flew along the kitchen to strike glancingly one wall, another, and finally stop almost at the feet of the girl who had fallen awkwardly across the doorstep, her long dress collecting in pools of chiffon about her. After a moment, not looking up, she reached for the shining bag and slipped the loop of it back about her wrist, as she sat there.

Louis glanced at the little gun in his left hand: the gun Weston had taken from her that morning and had yielded to Louis just before dinner.

"Did you really think," Louis asked, "that you could palm this from the sideboard upstairs, and neither Max nor Joseph nor I would notice it? What kind of comic-strip agents do you take us for?"

"It's my gun," she whispered. "It . . . was lying there. I just picked it up. It didn't *occur* to me you'd think . . ." She had said too much. She sensed it and stopped.

There was more between these two, Weston knew, than the question of a gun, even if she had meant, somehow, to use it; more than some expressed opinions that might be interpreted, from the tall man's point of view, as disloyal to him and the organization he stood for: after all, she could always claim she had been talking for Paul Weston's benefit, knowing quite well the microphones were there but never dreaming she would be taken seriously by those listening in upstairs. Weston tried to work it out; then Marilyn's shoulders moved in a tiny shrug and she rose and went outside without saying any more. At a gesture from Louis, Weston followed her.

It was dark on the iron stairs and darker down in the alley where a trickle of rain water ran like the stream at the bottom of a canyon. Louis indicated a door in the building opposite and suddenly they were indoors again, in a brightly lighted service corridor of some kind. They paused, at Louis's word, for Marilyn to run a comb through her hair and smooth down her dress; and the tall man gave them some further instructions, and a warning.

Walking through the lobby of the apartment house next door, with Marilyn beside him and Louis hovering protectively behind him, Weston could not make the place seem natural to him. He had got his shoes wet in the alley and it gave him a bedraggled feeling. He did not know where he was being taken or why; and he could not determine what his feelings ought to be about the girl at his side. He could not quite understand the attitude of the man behind him. It was as if he had suddenly come into a movie in the middle of the feature, and there was nobody to tell him what had gone before.

There was quite a bit of traffic in this building for that time of night: a laughing couple, quite young, went out ahead of them, while a middle-aged couple came in; and a woman wearing furs over a tailored suit waited by the door, presumably for her escort to bring the car around or return from parking it. She looked up as Weston and his companions approached; and he was sure that she was about to betray some surprise at the sudden appearance of two warmly-dressed young men accompanying a girl in a thin chiffon gown and not much else. It seemed to him that everyone who saw them must know that they did not belong here, and that there was something terribly wrong with the relationship between them. But the woman's glance, recognizing none of them, slid politely past them. It occurred to Weston that she might very well have saved her life, and his, by this reaction. For the first time he came to grips with the actual thought of the gun Louis would be holding ready in his pocket.

It had not been raining when they came down the fire escape, but it was raining softly when they stepped outside again now. Immediately, a car hissed up the gleaming drive to pick them up. The man in the brown suit, who had stood behind the bedroom door in the upstairs apartment, earlier in the evening, was at the wheel. He took them away from there fast; and as they turned into the wide street, beyond which were the trees of the park, there was a rending crash of metal from the left where one car, pulling out of a parking space, had been heavily rammed by another coming fast up the street. Weston was startled to recognize the ramming car as his own ancient sedan. A boy jumped out of it and darted across the street, losing himself in the park in an instant. The driver of the other car seemed stunned or hurt. Weston found the shock of seeing his own car wrecked replaced by a small growing sense of panic as he realized that this man must have been waiting there to follow them; and that Louis must have had a strong reason for having him so drastically put off their trail. It made Weston feel deserted and alone to know that there would be no help; he found that he had been vaguely counting on a rescue by somebody. They swung into a wailing right turn away from the park. Louis, kneeling on the front seat to watch the two in the rear, looked behind him.

"What about Max?" he asked, clearly referring to the boy who had run away.

"He'll be waiting down by the lakefront," the driver said. "I'm giving him time to get there; he's got almost a mile to go on foot."

"Where'd he get another car?"

"It was Bright Boy's." The man in the brown suit jerked his head toward Weston. "We jimmied the wheel lock and shorted the ignition. The heap wasn't good for much else."

Weston said automatically, "Hell, that was a good car." He felt a vague stirring of anger; the car he had just seen smashed had been his one major possession.

"Yeah," the driver said. "Ten years ago, it was a good car."

Marilyn's voice came out of the darkness beside Weston. "Who was in the other car?"

"Guess."

"The F.B.I. man?"

"Give the gold-plated garbage can to the little lady in the rear."

"I hate to interrupt this routine," Louis said. "But would you comedians mind shutting up?"

The nervousness implicit in this request for silence, from a man whom Weston would have guessed to be not often troubled with nerves, was more frightening than anything that had happened that evening.

When they swung out along the shore drive at last, the lake was lost in the wet darkness to the left. There had not been enough wind for the waves to be audible over the sound of the tires and the steady clicking of the windshield wipers; but somehow, even not seeing it or hearing it, you knew that the water was there. Louis had his gun in his hand now—a heavy, short-barreled revolver of a caliber large enough to give Weston the impression that, if the light should strike it right, he would be able to see down the wide bore to the bullet resting in the chamber. Something had changed, he knew; getting into this car had been a final step toward something to which Louis now felt himself committed. Weston could not make himself face the thought fully: it seemed too melodramatic and unreasonable.

The car turned into an opening in the screen of bushes to the right and coasted across a wide parking lot, well lighted and marked with neat painted lines. It was apparently too wet and too late at night for anyone to be using the beach which it served; and no couples seemed to have found it suitable for other purposes, perhaps because there was too much light, or because this was a weekday evening.

The windshield wipers kept up their steady beating after the car had been stopped. They waited, but nobody came out of the surrounding bushes to join them.

"Where the hell *is* the——?" Louis asked suddenly, using an epithet that seemed to shatter completely the illusion of gentility he had woven about himself earlier. The man in the brown suit said something reassuring. Louis said, "——him! We can't wait here all night." He waved the gun abruptly at the occupants of the rear seat. "Out, you!"

Weston reached for the door handle on his side. Behind him, he heard Marilyn's voice, surprised.

"Me?"

The drive seemed to have given her assurance; and her tone said that nothing that could happen to her would be more incredible than that, dressed as she was, she should be asked to get out into the rain in this deserted place.

"You, too, Elaine." There seemed to be a dry regret in the tall man's voice. Then something went shockingly wrong with it. *"All right! Move!"*

Weston's throat was suddenly tight and choked, his

chest constricted, as his body understood at last—before his mind would admit the fact—that he was going to be killed. *But why?* he asked himself desperately. It was clear now that Louis had come to the apartment to get him with this in mind, had brought him directly here for the purpose; but for what reason? The flawed note in the tall man's voice—his behavior throughout—said that for all his adventurous air he was no practiced killer. This was no movie where spies fired off guns at each other with reckless abandon: these were men trained in a certain line of work, one of the cardinal tenets of which was to avoid violence wherever possible, because violence attracted attention. *Then why?* Weston asked himself. Merely because he, and the girl still hesitating in the car behind him, had violated a sort of gangster code these people had? It did not seem likely they could afford such luxuries; but maybe they could.

Then Marilyn was standing on the wet pavement beside him in the yellow diffused light, in the rain, her hair instantly wet down her cheeks, the filmy layers of her evening gown quickly melting together to adhere unromantically to each other and to her. She seemed quite unaware of this or of the sudden wetness of her bare shoulders as she looked at him wide-eyed, having reached the same swift understanding that they were going to die.

The bushes crackled behind her and she started; and Weston instinctively braced himself to throw both of them to the ground, that being all he could think of doing if shooting started. But it was only the boy who had served dinner, who had smashed his car, soaking wet and breathless, stumbling out to them.

"——, it took you long enough!" Louis snapped, in that strained, inhuman voice.

"I got lost," the boy gasped. "It's like a ——ing jungle in there."

"Well, get in the ——ing car so you don't get lost again."

Louis gave Marilyn a little push and gestured to Weston. He was no longer a hearty man of the world; he was just a wet and worried—and therefore foul-mouthed—individual who had to kill a couple of people. Probably he had to do the job himself because neither of the others would take it on: murder was not in their contract, and they wanted no part of it. From the way Louis glanced back at them, Weston guessed that the tall man was not quite sure that they would not pull out and leave him. Then he gestured toward the bushes.

"Over here," he said.

"But—" Still not quite believing, Marilyn turned her head to protest.

"——you, get moving!" Louis seized on the excuse to let himself get angry. "You damn little bourgeois renegade!"

She went on, her bare shoulders a little hunched against the rain, carrying her now sodden dress in dripping handfuls about her knees while her silver sandals, still shining dully, splashed heedlessly through the pools of water on the pavement. The barrel of the gun poked Weston in the ribs. He thought of turning, swinging his arm back, as he had read it and seen it done in the movies; but before he could make up his mind to act, the touch was gone.

"In there," Louis said. "Tell her."

"Take the path," Weston said.

The disheveled girl ahead of him glanced around, startled at being addressed through him; then located the mouth of a path, blacker than the bushes that surrounded it, and turned in that direction. As the dark tunnel opened before him, so that he could see the light of the open field beyond, Weston knew that unless something happened they would never get through that darkness. *Quit stalling, you spineless jerk,* he told himself, *you might as well take it coming as going!*

The bushes were around him, brushing at him wetly. He could see Marilyn cringe from their contact with her skin, the whiteness of her shoulders a pale blur in front of him. He felt Louis close behind him. For a moment they were all together; and he dropped, sweeping Marilyn's feet out from beneath her with a kick that made her cry out with pain, as she fell and the gun crashed over their

71

heads. Louis, unable to stop in time, fell on top of them. They were threshing around in a hopeless confusion of limbs and wet clothes and angry, broken sounds of struggle; of hard pavement and soft earth and the resilient but impenetrable stalks of the bushes that responded to their bodies by showering them with water from above.

Suddenly Weston was free and up, and a gleam of bare arms told him Marilyn was clear and away up the path; between them, a formless shape struggled for a footing. He did not dare to close with it; simple fighting instinct told him that, killer or no, Louis outweighed him and outreached him and probably knew tricks he had never heard of. *Stay clear or he'll bend you like a pretzel!* he warned himself breathlessly, and kicked out with all his strength and again, feeling his foot strike solidly each time.

He felt no more compunction than if it had been a snake in the path. A hand caught his trousers leg; a pale oval the size of a face turned up to him; and he drove the hard leather heel of his other foot directly at the light target, striking with a terrible, unexpected accuracy, and feeling bone and cartilage smash beneath the blow. Free again, he hurdled the writhing body on the ground, and saw Marilyn, waiting, break into flight ahead of him. He found that he had not expected her to wait for him; seeing her still there was like receiving an undeserved present because somebody just happened to like you that well. It told him something about his feeling for her that he did not have time to stop and analyze. It almost let him forget the sickening crunch of his heel going home in Louis's face.

Somebody shouted and took a shot at them as they ran across the open field. Then there was brush all around them, and branches tearing them. The civilized city beyond the park, the handsome, well-dressed people they once had been, belonged to a dream world that had no relation to the desperate reality in which they now found themselves trapped. Later, Weston could not have said how long they ran, even after there was no longer anyone behind them.

IX

He stopped in the little tiled hallway to look at her in the light, while water drained from his own clothes to make pools on the floor. Outside, the rain splashed down unceasingly; and across the street he could see the dripping trees of the park out of which they had just come. She leaned against the mailboxes, breathless, covered to well below the knees by his drenched, muddy topcoat—a necessity, since there had been, in places, not enough left of her shockingly bedraggled chiffon gown to serve even the primary purposes of clothing. Below the coat, her bare legs were scratched, her feet bruised and muddy in the blackened, disintegrating evening sandals.

He said, "Well, we've obviously got to get clothes somewhere. If you've got any better ideas——"

"I just don't like begging clothes from your fiancée," she protested.

"She isn't any more," Weston said. "If that makes you feel better."

Marilyn glanced at him with weary puzzlement. "Well, she was last night when I picked you up in that bar, unless you were so tight you didn't know what you were talking about. You were afraid she'd get into trouble about it."

He said, "Well, she did in a way, and now she isn't. Not that I can see what that's got to do with——"

"Wait a minute." Marilyn frowned and straightened up, squeezing back her wet hair with both hands. There was an ugly scratch across her left cheek, and no make-up of any kind left on her face. He thought it was probably the first time he had ever seen her face completely bare of cosmetics; somehow it made her more of a person to him, and less of a romantic idea, than she had ever been. She looked younger, and it startled him to see that she looked intelligent; somehow he had never considered her intellectual capacity before, and her record certainly wasn't that of a particularly bright girl. Yet, on the other hand, you might say it was the brightest ones who were most in danger of being lured into crackpot crusades of one kind or another. "Wait a minute," she said, and there was a hard, questioning note to her voice that he had not heard before. "You've had just two chances to see her since last night and break the engagement. One, when you went home to change for dinner; and the other, while you were at that place—"

He said, "Damn it, what difference—"

"Louis said you'd murdered somebody there!"

"He said I was going to be arrested for it," Weston corrected her.

The tall girl facing him, with the naked, unfamiliar face and the squeezed-back wet hair, seemed to relax and even smile a little.

"I see. So *she* did it."

"I didn't say that," Weston protested.

"And you were going to take the blame for it?" After a moment, Marilyn said quietly, "You must be kind of in love with her, to want to shield her."

"Ah, shut up," he said uncomfortably. "Let's get some dry clothes before we start discussing romance."

"Can't I even talk about her?" Marilyn murmured.

He glanced at her irritably and poked a finger at the bell. A trickle of rainwater went down his spine as he moved, and it seemed to him that women picked the damnedest times for deciding who loved whom. A familiar voice came out of the tube, asking who was there. He thought it sounded frightened: Janie would be expecting the police. He gave his name and the buzzer let him open the glassed inner door for Marilyn, who went past him quickly and hurried up the stairs ahead of him, without looking back.

Janie was waiting for them on the third-floor landing, fully dressed. Light shone from the apartment door open beside her. Tonight, Weston thought, all the people he met seemed to have been too long in their clothes, too long awake. The small, dark-haired girl above him, he guessed, had not been to bed at all; she would have been waiting by the radio to hear that Dr. Lowery's body had been discovered. Even at a distance her print dress looked wilted and he thought that when he reached her he would find her eyes behind the shell-rimmed glasses pink, her face shiny with sleeplessness and fear.

She watched them come up the stairs toward her, with a little frown for Marilyn's costume that became a look of quick apprehension as Weston came into the light and she could see the state of his dinner jacket. But she did not speak, perhaps afraid to wake the occupants of the other apartments to this parade of scarecrows up the stairs. She stepped back to let Marilyn up to the landing, and the two girls faced each other awkwardly, waiting for Weston to reach them.

Then, as Weston mounted the last few steps to the landing, Marilyn held out her hand pleasantly enough and Janie took it; and the rest happened too quickly to be understood. Weston saw the two figures above him come together with abrupt violence, struggling for some object he could not see since it was hidden behind the taller girl, whose back was to him. There was a sharp, wicked crash of sound.

After a moment, Jane Collis backed away until the wall stopped her, staring at the small pistol in her hand. Her glasses had been knocked off in the struggle. Without them, her face had a startled, half-blind look. She glanced up abruptly and watched, fascinated, as the taller girl first steadied herself by the stairwell railing and then, quite slowly, crumpled to the floor. Then Janie looked at Weston.

"She . . . tried to kill me . . . !"

There was a brief instant in which he believed her. But the girl on the floor changed position slightly and was still again, her slow, pained breathing suddenly quite audible. He discovered a fierce relief at the knowledge that Marilyn was alive, mingled with a panic desire to know how badly she was hurt. He knew also that she had not tried to kill anybody; she had, instead, as once before

75

that night, stepped in the way to keep him from getting killed. It had been her way, he knew now, of repaying the debt she owed him. He did not need any evidence for this.

Janie was watching him. She could see him, all right, even without the glasses; she knew where to find him without trouble, but it was obvious that she could not read his expression. She peered at him through the mists of nearsightedness.

"Wes, she tried to kill me! She had a gun in her p—"

There was a dreadful little pause while she tried to decide whether to say purse or pocket. She looked down to see if the unconventionally dressed girl on the floor had even brought a purse. Momentarily diverted, her defective vision did not catch the start of Weston's movement in time; and before she could shoot he had struck the gun away from her. She cowered back against the wall, holding her hurt fingers to her mouth like a child. He wanted to strike her for what she had done, but the necessary rage would not come. Perhaps he was too tired.

"Not twice, Janie," he said. "I won't swallow that act twice in one night. You could kid me into thinking you'd killed Doc in self-defense, but now you're running the routine into the ground."

Then he was kneeling at Marilyn's side. She was still breathing very carefully, as if it hurt her. She made no sign that she knew he was there, and he did not speak to her. She had a silent battle of her own to fight, and he knew that she would not thank him for distracting her from the grim business of staying alive.

People, aroused by the shot, were moving uneasily behind the closed door facing Jane Collis's apartment. Rising, Weston knocked on the door. A man opened it. There was a woman behind him. Weston asked the woman to bring a blanket; and to cover and watch over the hurt girl while he called a doctor and the police.

He had the feeling of being on a stage speaking his lines too quickly just to get them out before he should forget them. The small girl backed against the wall gave him no help toward reality by beginning to curse him childishly; clumsily using epithets that were nasty and quite familiar. She did not sound like Jane Collis at all; but he had heard the same words in a man's mouth only an hour or so ago. The gun he had picked up was familiar also; it was Marilyn's little Colt automatic that had been passed from hand to hand all day, finally winding up in Louis's possession. Going in to telephone, herding Janie ahead of him, Weston found the tall man lying on the sofa in her tiny apartment, oblivious to everything but the agony of his smashed face.

Janie ran to him and went on her knees beside him and looked at Weston. "You lousy coward," she gasped. "To kick a man in the face like that! I wish I had killed you. I would have, if she hadn't interfered!"

Weston studied her for a moment, wanting to ask whether kicking a man in the face, as he had done to Louis, was worse than shooting him in the back, as Louis would have done to him; but it did not seem important. Holding the gun, he picked up the telephone left-handed, still watching them. Something in the way Janie looked at, and touched, the man on the sofa made the relationship between the two embarrassingly clear, and also the reason why Louis would run the risk of committing murder: to remove the one man beside himself who knew where Janie had been that night. For some reason, it seemed more shocking to think of little Jane Collis having a lover than to think of her being a spy or killing somebody.

X

They had to wait on a bench in the bare hospital corridor. Presently Richardson said, "I understand Acme is a little short of chemists right now. It's possible your Mr. French is going to have trouble finding men willing to work in a place that's been in the papers as a nest of spies.

I was talking to him this morning. You might try dropping around there when you're through here, if you're not too proud."

Weston nodded. It did not seem to him that he owed the big F.B.I. man any thanks, and the big man did not seem to expect any. A nurse in a starched white uniform went down the corridor to the door that had the right number, and inside. Presently she came back out and beckoned to them.

"Don't make her talk," the nurse said. "If you have any questions let her just answer yes or no."

"That's all right," Richardson said. "We've got it all pretty straight by now, anyway. How is she?"

"Oh, she's coming along very nicely," the nurse said.

Marilyn was lying in the white hospital bed, the only color in her face the fading ugly scratch she had got running through the park. She did not turn her head to greet them, but waited to smile at them until they had come to the foot of the bed where she could look at them without effort. Her lips formed a question.

Richardson said, "You're not supposed to talk. Louis is in the hospital. The little girl's in jail. We're waiting to see where the others run to before we pull them in." He watched the eyes of the girl in the bed. "Oh, him?" he said, glancing at Weston. "He's all right, I guess. I've just finished telling him his boss says he can have his job back. He doesn't seem very grateful."

Weston grinned. "Should I be? Maybe I should also thank you for using me as a stalking-horse in the first place."

"Well, we had to have some excuse to get into Acme without pointing a finger at the people we really suspected," the big man defended himself. "We wanted to see what would happen to that envelope. If you'd kept your temper you'd have been all right. But when you picked that moment, just when the mail was coming up the stairs, to start swinging iron bars around the place, it seemed like a little too much of a coincidence, if you get what I mean. When we realized the letter had vanished we knew you hadn't hidden it yourself—you hadn't had a chance—but it certainly looked as if you'd been trying to help whoever did get away with it. After that we couldn't gamble on explaining to you what we were trying to do. You didn't look like a good risk."

Weston said, "If you'd really wanted my cooperation, it might have helped to ask for it before you started playing games around the laboratory."

"Uhuh," Richardson said, "and also it might not, the way you were feeling about us. And besides, you're not a hell of a good actor, Mac."

"Well, you're not much of a detective," Weston said, "if you can't find an envelope taped under a desk drawer."

"We didn't want the envelope," Richardson said. "We wanted whoever had hidden it. The letter wasn't anything: hell, I wrote up those sheets of data myself, up at Faircraft. Why should I kill myself trying to find them?" He grinned at Weston's expression. "I was getting tired waiting for somebody to give me a break on this case, Weston. And too much information was going out through Acme. I don't know what they've told you about the Faircraft engine; actually, it's pretty hot stuff. I guessed that if I could get something in the works that was supposed to be the dope on it—and I had a line on their man at Faircraft and the code they were using—and then make them work like hell to get the information out, I'd learn something about who was passing the mail through Acme."

"They told me it wasn't very important," Weston said. He was aware of the girl in the bed watching them steadily, listening to their conversation; both men were a little uncomfortable, not knowing quite how to act in front of her. Weston found a strong tendency to drop his voice to a whisper, as if she were asleep. There was also a temptation to make her waste her strength answering stupid questions about how she was feeling and what she would like brought to her or done for her. And there was, finally, the urgent desire to get rid of the other man and speak to her alone. He found himself panic-stricken at the thought that the nurse might come back to send them away before he had had a chance to say what he had come here to say, that could not very well be said in front of anybody else.

Her lips formed a word. Richardson said, "Oh, the murder? Well, the plan was apparently that our mutual friend here—" he indicated Weston, "—would be sent into the plant to distract our attention, while the little girl escaped through the rear with the papers. Only, in the meantime, the chief chemist had caught her at the desk—he must have stayed behind to watch her, suspecting something—and she'd lost her head and killed him. Her sense of duty wasn't strong enough to let her face a murder rap just to get the papers out, so she persuaded Young Galahad on my right to take charge of both the papers *and* the murder, washing her hands of the whole thing. After she got home, I guess she began to worry about how far she could trust him to keep his mouth shut. So she called her boy friend to get rid of him, and you too, in case he'd whispered something to you."

Marilyn whispered, "She had the gun in her hand. When I came up the stairs. She tried to hide it in her dress. . . ."

Richardson said, "When Louis came staggering in with a bent profile—his pals dropped him at the door and lit out—and then the two of you turned up right on his heels, she must have figured Weston had caught on to the trick. She'd hoped, of course, that he'd be picked up leaving Acme with the papers on him and the body in the office. That would have fixed his clock so that nobody would have believed anything he said. But he wasn't quite that dumb."

Marilyn's eyes found Weston's face. She smiled a little. "He burned the papers," she whispered.

"Uhuh. Whether out of a sense of patriotism or self-preservation we'll never know," Richardson said, unimpressed.

" *I* know," she breathed.

"Yes," the big man said crossly. "You've known about him all along. Sure. But the rest of us don't happen to be in love with the guy." He turned abruptly away from the bed to face Weston; and when he spoke again, it was as if the girl was no longer in the room. "She's been working with us, you know," he said.

Weston did not say anything. He knew that what he was being told was extremely important; but it did not seem to matter. It was always too late for explanations. If you really needed an explanation you would not believe it; and when you were ready to believe it you no longer needed it.

Richardson said, "She came to us after a man in the State Department had killed himself. Later, we passed around the story that he'd left a note, to protect her in case anybody wondered where we'd got certain information. Actually, there hadn't been anything to connect her with the death except that she'd been one of several hundred people who'd known the man. But she walked in and told us exactly what she had been doing, and wanted us to tell her what it meant, and if there were anything she could do about it, or did we just want to put her in jail. We suspected her motives for a while because she held out your name and it wasn't hard to discover that she'd been seeing a lot of you. I'm afraid the boys in Washington made more trouble for you than they ordinarily would have, but you can see how it looked at the time, as if she were trying to shield you because you were guilty. . . ."

The girl in the bed moved slightly. Richardson did not look at her. There was a certain antagonism in his voice and attitude as he faced Weston; and Weston realized suddenly that the big man was, if not actually jealous, at least envious of him. It seemed to make the other man more human; and it seemed to bring the girl closer to him.

Richardson said, "Anyway, she's been working with us for two years. That's a long time for that kind of work. We knew they were getting suspicious of her when they sent her up here to make contact with you under circumstances where we almost had to pick her up; after all, we weren't even supposed to know where she was, and suddenly they were waving her in our faces. We seriously considered arresting her for her own protection, but she persuaded us not to." After a moment he turned toward the door, then paused. "Under the circumstances, I am authorized to say that the department sees no further reason for taking Miss George into custody, protective or otherwise." Then he was gone, gently closing the door behind him.

Marilyn turned her head slowly, watching Weston come along the side of the bed toward her. He stopped and stood looking down at her where she could still see him comfortably. There was an awkward pause; and what he said at last was not at all what he had planned.

"Look," he said, "what the hell is your name, anyway?"

"Marilyn," she whispered. "Elaine was just a code name they used." After a while she said, "Don't be grateful, Paul. Even if I did in a way save your life, you still haven't exactly gained by knowing me."

"That," he said, "is what you think."

THE BLACK CROSS

I

When he got her out to the car at last she said she was quite able to walk and he did not have to drag her. So he let go her arm and she stood for a moment, smoothing the white silk jersey of her dress over her hips; no man was going to rush her and especially not a husband. Then she got into the car. It seemed as if all of them were standing on the porch watching, except Chris, who had run inside.

He started around the car to get behind the wheel and the lights came on and the motor started. She was sitting waiting for him with her foot on the gas and the cold, stubborn look on her face that he knew very well; and there was really no point in making any further exhibition of the Phillips family that evening, so he went back and got in beside her. She took them out of there so fast that they were doing fifty when they hit the road at the rustic sign that said *The Larches, J. and V. Cunningham.* Hugh Phillips had always suspected that Jack and Vivian thought they were referring to a species of bird when they put it up, since there was not a tree on the place that was even close.

"I'm not drunk," Janice said.

Hugh Phillips did not say anything. There really wasn't any point in arguing about it.

"I'm not a bit drunk," she said. "I'm not even high. I just got tired of watching her trailing you around. Ever since we came down here she's been trailing you around, and if nobody else will put her wise to the fact that you're married, then I will."

He sat beside her remembering the way Christine Wells's face had become more and more pale until he was afraid that she would faint or begin to cry, either of which would have been completely dreadful. She had looked at him, begging him silently to stop it; but you did not stop Janice except by force once she had started to blow her top about something; and in the final analysis he had already, a year ago, made his choice between Janice and Christine Wells. He could not make Janice look ridiculous by carting her off the porch on his shoulder: she was his wife. She was making a damn fool of herself and she was hurting Christine quite unjustly and the whole thing was a mess, but he was still married to her.

They bounced over the country road at a fantastic speed, and at the main highway where the direction markers said Washington was sixteen miles to the left, they shot away to the right toward Annapolis. The speedometer climbed to seventy and Janice's mouth looked dark and reckless in the glow of the dashboard. Her face was almost classical in profile, the dark hair braided up tightly to show the fine shape of her head. There was a flat pearl disc in the lobe of her ear.

She had got herself a deep smooth tan that spring, and the rich color of her neck and arms was barbaric against the draped silk jersey of the white dress. It was never any use for him to ask himself how he had come to marry her, because these days the answer was always right there when he looked at her. Even the way she had dressed when he first met her at the University, the men would turn around when she walked through the office where she worked; and nowadays she left hardly anything to the imagination. He had not yet figured out why being married to him should give her a sudden desire for extreme clothes, when most faculty wives became dowdy in short order. He consoled himself with the thought that it would have been too bad to have a wife who acted like a bitch and looked like hell, too.

"Well, say it," Janice said abruptly.

"Say what?"

"Tell me I acted like a bitch. That's what you're thinking, isn't it?"

Sometimes her guesses were disconcertingly accurate. "Let's just skip it," he said. "Let's skip the whole thing."

"I love you when you're magnanimous," Janice said.

At seventy the Ford went into nasty little crabwise hops on the curves, and on the straightaways it seemed to rise up and float an inch or two off the ground, occasionally dropping back to earth with a jar. The headlights picked out a sign saying Washington was twenty-two miles behind them; it was gone in an instant. Janice reached out and turned on the radio. Presently she began to croon softly to the music, to tell him how little his opinion of her disturbed her.

"And I don't mean to be critical of your friends," she said, "but don't you know anybody who drinks scotch or bourbon? For heaven's sake sit still. Don't wiggle."

"Watch the road," he said. "If you're going to drive like a fool, don't look at me, watch the road."

"Don't tell me how to drive."

"Somebody should tell you."

"It's my car. If I want to wreck it, I'll wreck it."

"All right," he said. "But let me out first."

She began to sing again. She was always singing. It was enough to drive a man crazy when he was trying to study; other times it could be rather pleasant, when she went up to the radio and sang along with the music, to him, in that personal kind of way she had. . . . It was not exactly what one expected from marriage, but it was pleasant. But there were times when the singing and the radio made him want to kill her.

She stopped singing and put the gas pedal to the floorboards as the inside of the car filled with light from behind; then a three-tone horn waved them aside and a big car passed them as if they were standing still. Janice spoke a sharp ugly word; she hated to be passed. They could see the twin tail-lights of the big car taking the curves ahead of them, and occasional headlights whipped past on the way to Washington, but at that time of night the traffic was sparse.

"I mean," Janice said, "it's either gin or some lousy blend that nobody ever heard of, and then they come over to our place and swill Old Grand-dad like it was Coca-Cola."

The draft from the hood ventilator had blown her skirt back into her lap, and Hugh Phillips had had enough to drink, himself, that he found this interesting, even if it was his wife.

"It's not like during the war when you couldn't get the stuff," she said. She glanced at him and smiled a little, and brushed the skirt negligently into place. "Well, I'm glad you still like my *legs,* at least," she murmured.

Then they hit the curve down to Littlefish Creek, and there was a moving van with a flat tire parked on the road; and a car was just passing it, coming up from below. There wasn't enough space left to take a motorcycle through.

"Did your wife always drive when you rode together?" the black-haired man asked. Hugh Phillips watched him idly and thought that he should have been wearing a bright plaid shirt and hobnail boots and singing a song in French-Canadian dialect against a technicolor background. Instead he wore a very fine gabardine suit and had a notebook on his knee.

"Usually," Phillips said. "You see, it was her car."

The black-haired man glanced up from the notebook.

"I mean," Phillips said, "she had it before we were married. That made it her car."

Everything was quite clear of the parts he could remember, but he could not remember all of it. But he could see himself lying down against the side of the wrecked car with the windshield six inches in front of his face and the steering wheel above him; and above that the open door gaping to the sky. There were stars in the sky and he could see the top of a tree. The radio was still playing. He wanted to turn it off. One headlight at least was still burning, showing him, through the splashed windshield, the upward slope to the road with the trees and bushes shattered by their decent.

The car rocked a little and he heard her sobbing outside as she tried to climb up what had been the bottom and was now the side, to reach him, and he could not make himself speak to her. He could only say over and over to himself, "Dear God, please God, don't let the damn thing start to roll again. Don't let it turn over again. . . ."

The hospital room was clean and bright with daylight and a Maryland state policeman stood by the door.

"You didn't think it was dangerous to let her drive in her condition?" the black-haired man asked.

"She wasn't drunk," Hugh Phillips said. "She'd just had enough to make her stubborn. I didn't think it was important enough to argue about. She'd always got us home all right before."

They were just talking about a girl named Janice that both of them knew.

"You'd had a fight, hadn't you?" the black-haired man asked.

"Not exactly. She objected to my talking to a girl at the party."

"Did you continue the fight on the way home?"

Hugh Phillips shook his head.

"Did you have any more to drink while you were driving?"

Hugh Phillips shook his head.

"Did you stop anywhere along the road?"

Hugh Phillips shook his head. He was working on the parts that were missing.

"She's dead, isn't she?" he asked.

"Don't you remember? You told Sergeant Case when he arrived. . . ."

The state policeman moved a little. Apparently he was Sergeant Case.

When she came into the light her hair had come down and her left arm was scraped and bleeding from the naked shoulder to the elbow, and her left thigh from the bared smudged girdle to the knee; the white dress almost completely ripped away on that side. She had lost her white pumps and she was covered with motor oil. She swayed a little from shock and hurt and gave the man hell for parking his truck on the pavement beyond a blind curve. He thought that no man had a right to see his wife like that, and he had better get out there and put a coat on her.

"Tell me how it happened," the black-haired man said.

"Who are you?"

"Holt. From the sheriff's office."

Hugh Phillips said, "We came around the curve at fifty something, and the truck was parked there . . ."

"Heading down?"

Phillips nodded. ". . . and a car coming up was just passing it. There wasn't any place else to go, so we went over. Where am I?"

"You're in the Emergency Hospital in Annapolis."

For a while he had not been anywhere. Being in Annapolis put him back into the world again, so to speak, and he knew what things would look like when he got outside. There would be old brick houses, and midshipmen from the Naval Academy on the streets in the late afternoon, and he could drop into the Tap Room at Carvel Hall for a drink, but he would have to do it alone.

He remembered the state policeman asking questions while the doctor patched him up in the light of a flashlight. Then some men came along with a stretcher and loaded him on top of it and the doctor stuck a hypodermic in his arm. When he woke up it was daylight and they had cleaned him up and put him into a hospital nightgown. He tried his arms and legs and they worked. He could see and hear. He was in fine condition. Another doctor came in to tell him so. He was a very lucky man, the doctor said. In spite of the fine condition he was in he hurt all over.

The black-haired man asked a question.

"Yes, I'm quite sure she was driving," Hugh Phillips said. The missing parts were flooding back and he did not like them. He wanted to get them out and done with—referred for action to the proper authorities, as you said during the war when you wanted to pass the buck. It did not seem to him that it made any difference who was driving.

"Have you got the truck-driver yet?" he asked, and the voice that came out, remembering, suddenly belonged to somebody else. It was raw and savage, and startled him, because he did not feel like that about it at all. He just wanted to know if they had got him yet.

"No, we're looking for him." Mr. Holt closed his note-book and ran his hand over his smooth black hair. They pushed something with rubber tires down the hall outside, talking. The black-haired man glanced at Sergeant Case and said reluctantly, "There was something about a cross, wasn't there? You told Sergeant Case . . ."

"Yes," Hugh Phillips said. It was very clear now. "A black cross. He hit her with it. Then he kneeled beside her and hit her again. With the cross. Then he went back up to the truck and drove away." He could see that they did not believe a word of it.

II

In the afternoon Sergeant Case brought a girl in to see him. She came in sideways and stood against the wall by the door, a little round-shouldered and awkward with embarrassment and uneasiness. She wore a gray flannel suit and a pink shirtwaist that tied in a bow under her chin. The state policeman said that her name was Shirley Carlson and that she had been driving the other car. Shirley Carlson said she was dreadfully sorry about the whole thing. Hugh Phillips said it was not her fault at all, and that made her feel a little less uncomfortable, but not much. She went out of the room with the state policeman. Presently Mr. Holt came in.

Mr. Holt came across the room and sat down on the bed lighting a cigarette, holding out the package as an after-thought. He had a powerful catlike body and his face had the impersonal handsomeness of a wood carving and the color of old mahogany. When he moved, the fine gabardine suit he was wearing seemed thin and fragile to contain the energy inside it.

"She backs you up that your wife was driving," Mr. Holt said. "You're pretty lucky, kid."

Hugh Phillips said, "Yes. Jan is dead, the car's smashed and I've got nine stitches in my leg. Everything is breaking right for me. Some days you can't lose." He refused the cigarettes.

"That was a nasty gash you had," Mr. Holt said. "For a while I wondered why there wasn't any more blood in the car."

"I must have got it when I started pulling myself out of there," Phillips said.

The black-haired man nodded. "I figured that out after a while. You must have been pretty much in love with her to want to get to her that badly. If you'd waited . . ."

"I couldn't just lie there looking at her."

"How long had you been married?"

"A year this fall." He took a cigarette after all, and the smoke hurt his bruised lip. "She was working in the office at Johns Hopkins when I came back from the service. I had her do some typing for me. She was a lousy typist."

"You're a professor at Hopkins?"

"Thanks," Phillips said. "Instructor. Sociology."

"I wouldn't have picked her as the wife of a college teacher," the black-haired man said idly.

"Well, I did," Phillips said stiffly. After a moment he went on, "I guess she'd never felt free to spend money on herself before. She told me she had supported her parents until they died and I guess she had just got into the habit of living on hardly anything. She had quite a bit saved up. I couldn't say anything when she started to spend it. I didn't want to. Things were pretty dull for her, anyway. I hadn't taught much before, and they gave me a heavy schedule so I didn't have time for much except studying. I didn't really mind as long as she was having fun, although I'll admit that some of the things she bought looked a little startling on campus." He smiled. "On the other hand, a man gets kind of a kick out of suddenly discovering that his wife is a knockout. I mean, in the office she was a nice-looking kid with good legs, but her figure could have been anything in the clothes she used to wear. . . . Of course, I looked her over on the beach before I decided to marry her," he added, grinning quickly, and then he stopped grinning, annoyed with himself for telling a stranger things about his private life that were none of the man's business.

"Did she often drink as much as last night?" the black-haired man asked.

"She hadn't had much," Phillips said defensively. Then he gave in. "Well, she did drink more than I liked to, at least lately. Just the last few weeks. She hated it down here and said it bored her to death. . . . We were put out of our apartment in Baltimore," he explained in answer to the black-haired man's look. "The folks gave us the summer place on the bay until we could find something else."

"Is there any relative of hers you want to notify?"

He shook his head. "She had some people on the West Coast, but I never met them and as far as I know she never wrote to them. I wouldn't know how to get in touch with them."

"What do you want to do about the funeral?"

"My mother's coming down from Baltimore," Phillips said wearily. "Talk to her, will you? I don't know much about funerals."

While he had been talking about her it had seemed for a moment as if Janice were alive again, and losing that feeling left an emptiness inside him.

The black-haired man got up and walked to the window. Phillips watched him without interest. He did not dislike the man because the man would not believe him, but he wished he could be alone and not have to talk about it; and his leg and head both hurt.

"I know what you're thinking, kid," Mr. Holt said without looking around. "You think your wife was murdered and we're not doing a thing about it. You're wrong. We'll catch the man and if we don't like his story . . ."

He turned slowly, sitting down on the sill. "Look at it from my point of view, Phillips. The state police call me because a car has gone off the road and a man says his wife was murdered. With a cross, mind you. A black cross!"

Hugh had been thinking, and he knew all about it. "Would it help any if I called it a socket wrench?" he asked.

Mr. Holt looked up quickly.

"He was fixing a tire," Phillips said. "He was changing a tire and he had one of these big four-way wrenches to take the nuts off. When he ran down there he carried it with him. He probably didn't even realize he had it. . . ."

"Are you sure or are you guessing?"

"What else would a man like that be using that looked like a cross?"

The black-haired man nodded. "All right. You're probably right, kid," he said slowly. "But where does that get us? You still called it a cross when they found you. That shows your condition." He got up and came to the bedside table to crush out his cigarette. Then he stood over the bed, smiling a little. "I want to tell you the way I had it figured out first," he said wryly, "so that you can see I'm not afraid to admit when I'm wrong. I saw a car that had gone off the road and a girl who could have smashed her head on a rock when she was thrown clear; and I asked myself, now why would the kid want to call it murder? Then I checked with the folks you had been visiting . . ."

"That must have been interesting," Phillips murmured.

". . . and I started to thinking about a young married couple quarreling," the black-haired man went on. "He starts to get behind the wheel and she beats him to it. They drive off practically tearing up the road. The people in the house can smell rubber burning clear back from the gate. The young man doesn't go for this so he makes his wife change places with him. . . . All right, but it could have happened. He was mad, they were both mad. They were at least a little tight; I couldn't get anybody to admit you were pie-eyed, but you'd both had a couple and then another couple. . . . Well, they keep on fighting and presently the husband starts trying to scare the wife by crazy driving. . . ."

Hugh Phillips laughed abruptly.

"It could have happened," the black-haired man said calmly. "I've seen it happen. And then you go off the road and when you wake up she's dead and your conscience tells you that you as good as killed her. You feel like a murderer and you've had a crack on the head and the thing that pops into your mind is that you're going to be blamed for it if you can't pin it on somebody else. You see the truck-driver with his socket wrench. He beats it because he thinks that you're both dead and he'll be blamed for leaving his truck like that. You stagger up to the road and tell everybody the truck-driver killed your wife with a black cross. Just to make it fancy."

The big man laughed pleasantly. "It was a nice pipe-dream," he said. "The Carlson girl knocks it on the head. Your wife *was* driving. But I just wanted to show you that I've had some reason for the silly questions I've been asking."

It seemed to Hugh Phillips that this was largely irrelevant. He could not feel concerned over the possibility that he might have been suspected of concealing manslaughter in what appeared to be a remarkably stupid manner.

"She was wearing a white dress," he said. "There wasn't much left of it but she had got it pretty well covered with motor oil and grease. If she . . ." He swallowed. "If she died instantly, how did she get back to the car to get her dress so dirty?"

"There was oil all down the hillside, kid," the black-haired man said gently. "Your oil line must have gone the minute you started to roll. And besides . . ." He hesitated. "Oil and blood look pretty much alike at night," he said.

"On her hands, too," Phillips said absently. He looked up. "I know what I saw, Mr. Holt. I'm just trying to find something to convince you. She had it all over her hands. How would she get that, just being thrown clear? I'm trying to show that she must have been alive afterward. Wasn't there . . . Didn't you find her footprints?"

Mr. Holt said, "She'd lost her shoes, remember, and when I got there a dozen people had been tramping up and down the slope. Not much chance of finding tracks of a girl in her stocking feet. Sorry. And there wasn't much oil on her hands."

"I know. I wiped them off. With my handkerchief."

"You didn't happen to wipe your own hands with the same handkerchief, did you, kid? Before . . . ?"

Hugh Phillips sighed. It was no use at all and he let himself sink back to the pillow. "I guess I did. When I touched her . . . I'd got it all over me, climbing out. I wiped my hands and then hers and . . . and fixed her up a bit and put my coat over her. I guess I was crying. I don't remember. I left her there with the light on because it seemed better than leaving her in the dark. Did I get all the way up to the road?"

The black-haired man nodded. "You walked right out in front of a car. Scared the man to death; he had to go up on the cutbank to miss you."

"Bleating about a black cross," Hugh Phillips said bitterly. "That's what gets you, isn't it? The black cross."

Mr. Holt nodded again. "It shows you weren't exactly in your right mind, doesn't it, kid? The way we figure it now, you heard the truck-driver trying to get into the car. Your first thought was your wife, naturally, and you wanted her to be all right so badly that you jumped to the conclusion it was she. You weren't thinking very clearly, but you got it fixed in your mind that she was alive; and then you looked around and saw her lying there and this man was kneeling beside her holding this wrench that he had forgotten about. You assumed hazily that he had killed her." He spread his hands. "Why should he kill her, Phillips? Give one good reason! It doesn't make sense."

The story sounded so plausible that he found himself wondering if it had not really happened that way, and when he answered, his reasoning seemed far-fetched and improbable.

"He was rattled. He knew he had no business leaving his truck like that; and then a girl comes at him out of the darkness looking like she did in that white dress and bawling him out hysterically, accusing him of having killed me. . . ." Everything that happened to Janice was always somebody else's fault, he remembered wryly. "He just swung with whatever he had in his hand; and then he had to finish the job."

The black-haired man was no longer interested. "If that's what you really think happened . . . I mean if you really saw it like that, then it's your right to make a statement and it will be put in evidence against the man when we catch him," he said. Then he sat down on the bed and slowly produced another cigarette and lighted it. "It's your right," he said. "But I'm advising you not to exercise it, Phillips."

"Why?"

The older man glanced at him. "I know quite a bit about murder, kid," he said. "Before you get yourself out on a limb, I want you to remember that murder is something you can't stop once it gets started, and it's also something you never get away from, once it has touched you. In other words, you make your statement, we catch the man, and you've got to go through with it or admit you were seeing things. If you go through with it your story won't stick. The first thing the defense will do is put your statement to Sergeant Case in evidence: *My wife was killed by a man wielding a black cross*. Period. That washes you up. You say it was a socket wrench. Defense attorney asks when did you decide it was a socket wrench. You say you decided it talking to Mr. Holt of the sheriff's office." Mr. Holt smiled. "Take it from there, kid."

"Yes," said Phillips dryly. "I get it, all right. In other words I can see a man kill my wife and because I don't happen to pick on the right name for a certain tool the murderer goes free. . . ."

"Not necessily," Mr. Holt said. "It just casts a certain doubt on your standing as a witness, don't you see? I'm not arguing with you for your own good, I'll admit," he went on, smiling. "We don't want the papers heckling us about a murder we can't prove even happened since the only witness is a young fellow who had a pretty nasty crack on the head. Furthermore we want this man for leaving the scene of an accident, and we've got a damn sight better chance of getting him if he doesn't hear that he's wanted for murder, too. Finally, we've got plenty of work to do without wasting time on a case that's going to be thrown out of court. That's one side of the picture, Phillips," the black-haired man said, standing up again beside the bed. "The other is this: I've heard your story. I won't say I believe it, but you can bet your boots I won't forget it. We're going to get that lad and when we get him I'm going to grill him, personally."

There was a peculiar quality to his smile and to the small wrist movement with which he flicked ashes at the tray on the table.

"I'm pretty good at that, kid," he said softly. "If there's a crack in the man's story, I'll find it. I don't like murder any more than you do. It's my business not to like it. I'll be watching for it. If the guy killed your wife like you say, I'll get it out of him. . . ."

"And then," said Phillips evenly, "my evidence won't be any good because they'll want to know why I didn't sing out sooner."

Mr. Holt said, "You make your statement, notarized, and keep your mouth shut at the inquest. I keep the statement in the sheriff's safe. If we do find the man did it I'll say that we were withholding your evidence so that the man would not get spooked and leave the country."

"I don't like it," Hugh Phillips said. "I want to get up in court and say that my wife was murdered."

"No, you don't," Mr. Holt said. "You know you don't. Nobody wants to have anything to do with murder. You just feel you ought to."

Phillips was silent.

"I didn't finish telling you about murder," the black-haired man said. "I said, it's something you don't ever get away from, once it's touched you. I think you're feeling what I mean right now. You'd rather not mess with it, but you have to. You'd a damn sight rather she'd just died in the accident, wouldn't you?"

Phillips nodded.

"I don't want to give the impression of trying to scare you," Mr. Holt said gently. "I'm just telling you what will happen if you insist on forcing us to call it murder. Remember that you'd been quarreling with your wife and that people knew you didn't get along too well. . . ."

"We got along fine," Phillips said, and it seemed strange to realize that they actually hadn't. "We got along beautifully except when she played the radio too loud."

"Yes," said Mr. Holt, "but other people had a different impression. When we catch this man, the murder charge won't stick, assuming that no new evidence shows up. And pretty soon people will start to remember that the last anybody saw both of you together you were both pretty mad at each other. There won't be any evidence against you and nothing will ever be done about it, but people will wonder just why you were so hot to hang the poor man. They'll remember murder against you, oh, very vaguely: *Wasn't there something about his wife? That's right, she was murdered; anyway, that's what he said.* Did she have any insurance?"

"No."

"But she had been spending money pretty freely, and all you had was an instructor's salary?"

"That's right. So I killed her to keep her from spending her own money."

"I didn't say it," the black-haired man murmured, smiling. "I didn't even think it. I'm just telling you the way people in general think. You don't want to start this unless you can finish it, and you can't."

"You're pretty hot to have me keep quiet, aren't you?" Hugh Phillips said harshly.

The black-haired man laughed cheerfully and buttoned the coat of his gabardine suit. "Think it over and you'll see I haven't said anything that isn't the truth, kid. As far as I'm concerned, as far as the old man's concerned, we don't feel justified in making a murder charge on the evidence we've got; and we don't want a lot of shouting in the papers. It's just the same with us as with you, they'll remember it against us as another unsolved case even if we catch the man and bring him to trial, because he'll be acquitted and that'll leave us with a murder case and no suspect." He stroked his black hair. "I'll send in a stenographer and you make your statement. We'll hold it. What you say at the inquest is your own business. Nobody's going to coerce you." At the door he turned. "Would you say you could identify the man, kid?"

Hugh Phillips sat very still for a long moment. Then he said slowly, "Yes, I'll know him."

As the door closed he frowned, wondering why he had lied. The man had been only a dark shape in coveralls holding the wrench and a flashlight; and if they ever asked him to pick out Janice's murderer from a row of men he would have to admit that it could be any or none of them, that the murderer could come up to him and ask him for a match and he would never know the difference.

But there were two people in the world who knew how Janice had died, and he had served notice on the other. Because if Hugh Phillips could identify the man, he must have seen him; and if he had seen him, the man would know that he had also seen him kill her. There was a vague chance that he might want to do something about it other than get as far away from Phillips as possible. There were times when you had to stick your neck out a little way.

Hugh Phillips looked at the mirror above the dresser at the foot of the bed. The face in the mirror had a black eye, freckles, a swollen lip, and a lump of adhesive tape a little back from the right temple where the short reddish hair had been shaved away to make room for it. The face still looked younger than its twenty-six years in spite of its battered condition. He felt years older than the face, but when he lay back on the pillow it vanished below the frame of the mirror, so apparently it belonged to him. He had never been so lonely in his life and there was nobody he wanted to see except one person, and she would not come.

He hoped she would forgive him for doing what the black-haired man wanted.

III

He waited until the courtroom had cleared before he moved toward the door, still feeling rather weak and fragile and not equal to being shoved around by a crowd of people. He felt a great sense of relief at having the inquest over with. It could not have been more routine; everything had gone the way the black-haired man would have wanted it, and it was a little surprising that he had not turned up to see it; but the doctor and the state policeman named Case had said all that needed to be said. Then the coroner had made a little speech about liquor and gasoline not mixing very well; and he had verbally patted Miss Shirley Carlson on the head for her quickness in notifying the police, and censured the absent truck-driver for his disappearance. The police had come in for a dose of gentle sarcasm: it was a little strange, the coroner had said, that a moving van complete with driver could vanish without trace in the Free State of Maryland. The coroner had been kind to Hugh Phillips: if the bereaved husband had not learned his lesson from tragic experience, he had said, then words would be futile. He had directed that the truck-driver be charged with criminal negligence and leaving the scene of an accident; and that Mr. Phillips keep himself available to identify the man when apprehended.

Outside it was bright sunshine and Phillips stood for a moment, while people walked past him, squinting down the long dazzling flight of stone steps ahead of him. It would, he thought, be damned silly if he were to fall down them and break his fool neck, but he did not feel at all sure of getting down safely. For a moment he regretted having insisted on his parents' leaving; but it would have looked too ridiculous for a grown man to bring his folks into court with him, like a small boy caught throwing stones at the grammar school windows. He wondered where he could find a taxi and if he had enough money with him to cover the ride to Sand Point. Well, there was money in the house. He found himself still standing at the head of the steps, a little afraid to start down.

"Is anything wrong?"

He turned sharply and saw the girl who had driven the other car coming out of the shade of the building behind him. She was wearing a yellow silk dress printed with black; and the thin dress, and the high heels she was wearing, made her body seem all legs. *Well, if you like the coltish type,* Janice would have said. Other women always reminded Janice unflatteringly of domestic animals. The girl had soft brown hair and a fresh snub-nosed face.

"Can I . . . do you feel all right?" she asked uncertainly.

He was suddenly afraid that she was going to take his arm as if he were an invalid. He turned and started down the steps, and heard her heels, after a moment, rapping a little unevenly on the stones behind him. When he glanced back she was flushing, trying to act as if she were coming out of the courthouse quite alone: she thought he had deliberately snubbed her.

"I realize you'd rather not talk to me," she said stiffly, reaching him. "I'm sorry I . . ."

"Nuts," he said.

"I'm not a very good driver," she said breathlessly. Her heels made two quick taps on the steps, and then she waited for him, and then two more and another pause while he took the steps slowly, one at a time. "I've been hating myself for being so stupid, Mr. Phillips," she said, and he could see that she had saved all this up to tell him if she could get the chance. "If I'd had the sense to pull out to the side when I saw your lights . . . But you were coming so fast, and I couldn't think of anything except slamming on the brakes and . . . and just sitting there with my silly mouth open. . . ." Her heels tap-tap-tapped on the stone steps as he got a little ahead of her. It was like waiting for water to drip from a faucet.

Hugh Phillips said irritably, "Listen, we were coming around that corner practically on two wheels, Miss Carlson. She couldn't have turned any sharper if she'd had the state of Texas over there to shoot at; we'd have rolled right over. The truck fixed us. You didn't have a thing to do with it. It wasn't your fault and would you mind not talking about it. . . ." He felt himself go red. "I'm sorry," he said.

She was silent and the heels settled to a sedate crisp rhythm beside him. On the sidewalk she stopped to face him.

"Can I drive you anywhere? My car's right around the corner."

He shook his head. "It's 'way out in the sticks. I'll take a taxi."

"Where?"

"Out near Rio Vista."

"That's only a couple of miles past our place," she said, making it a statement, not urging him.

He hesitated and shook his head again. "I . . . want to take a look at something first, Miss Carlson. Thanks a lot, anyway."

"Yes," she said slowly, "of course." Then she frowned. "But I thought your parents took . . . her up to Baltimore . . . one of the policemen told me. . . ." She was quite pink and tongue-tied. She thought he was going to look at Janice's grave.

He said flatly, "That's right. They did."

"Oh," she said, and the color faded from her face. She studied him for a moment. "You're going . . . out *there?*"

He nodded. "Gruesome, ain't it?"

She drew a deep breath. "Let me drive you, please. I'd feel I had at least done something to help. . . ."

"All right," he said, and they walked around the corner to her car, a new Pontiac sedan. "Lucky girl," he said, sitting back against the cushions as she sent the car away from the curb.

She glanced at him. "Oh, the car? Yes, isn't it lovely?"

"I'm going to have to get something to drive, living out there," he said. "I can't see myself hiking five miles for groceries with this leg."

"You're staying on, then?"

"I've still got a bunch of courses to work up." After a moment he said, "Of course, you know you saved my neck, Miss Carlson."

She looked startled. Then she laughed. "Oh, you mean when that man wanted me to say that you were driving?"

"He tried to get you to say that?"

"Not really. I mean, he didn't actually *tell* me . . . You know what I mean."

"It's lucky for me you saw it." Hugh Phillips grinned. "As far as I was concerned, King Kong could have been driving this car." He glanced at her, toying with an idea he had had before. "Did I look scared?"

Shirley Carlson laughed, watching the road unwind ahead of them. They were leaving the outskirts of Annapolis.

"I'm afraid I didn't notice you, Mr. Phillips. I was looking at the driver, I guess to see what she was going to do. I thought for a moment she was going to turn right toward me. I sort of subconsciously noticed that it was a girl. . . ."

"The hair," he said.

The girl nodded. "I guess so. I just knew it was a girl, that's all, so when he asked me . . ."

"Jan had her hair up," Hugh Phillips said quietly. "She always pulled it up tight when she wanted to look real slick. And I mean tight, just a couple of braids across her head."

He could feel his heart beating strongly as he waited for the girl in the yellow dress to answer. It had seemed to him almost impossible that in the moment the headlights, never dimmed, flashed around the curve and over the shoulder into the trees, Miss Shirley Carlson could have noticed the sex of the driver. Yet there was no good reason why she should have put herself out to help him; and she might have noticed it as you do notice some one thing when you are very frightened; and if so he was making a fool of himself and being very rude to a girl who had done her best to be nice to him.

The car came to a gentle halt beside the road; and as it stopped he began to hear the crickets in the bright field beyond the fence to the right.

"It's not very nice of you to play detective," Shirley Carlson's voice said. "It's not very nice of you to trick me, Mr. Phillips. I came back with them and saw you being carried away, and *her,* and they told me she was dead. It seemed a little unnecessary that you should have any more trouble, so when the man asked me I said that she had been driving. . . . I don't know who was driving, Mr. Phillips," the girl said breathlessly, "but it seems to me now that the only way you could *know* I was lying . . ." She was abruptly silent. "Now *I'm* playing detective," she said at last, and started the car forward again.

The road was black and shimmering with heat in the sunshine, and he watched it wind away ahead of them.

"I don't want to know," the girl said stiffly. "Please don't tell me."

"I remembered that I hadn't seen you," he said. "All I saw was headlights. And Jan with her hair up . . . well, her head got a funny boyish look, I mean funny considering that she was about the least boyish-looking girl you could imagine. If you just caught a glimpse of it I couldn't see how you could tell, to swear to it." He grimaced. "I'm sorry, Miss Carlson. I should have kept my big mouth shut."

"It's all right," the girl said without taking her eyes from the road.

"Please," he said. "I'm grateful as hell. And she was driving."

Shirley Carlson smiled at last. "Well, it *was* mean of you to trick me," she said.

When they came to the place there was nobody at all around, and the tire tracks in the earth cutbank where the man had driven out to avoid Hugh Phillips when he stumbled out on the road that night were blurred with the rain of a past thundershower. There was only the smooth sharp curve of the highway leading out of sight in front of them. When a car came around it they both sat very still in the parked sedan and watched it, as if expecting to see it hurtle over the edge into the trees, but it went on, and the sound of it died behind them.

"I'll be back in a minute," Phillips said.

The girl nodded, her eyes thanking him for not asking her to go with him. He limped across the road and saw the broken bushes below him, but everything seemed to be growing back very quickly. The rain had helped, but it seemed as if the woods were hastening to hide the scar. The car was gone. It had been hauled out the next day, his mother had told him, and a junk-man had taken it. It was the insurance company's business, anyway.

He went down and kicked among the leaves, some still oilstained. Everything looked different in daylight; and it was difficult to remember how far it had seemed to the road after he had left her lying there that night. He wandered back among the trees and found a white high-heeled pump among the dead stuff on the hillside. The suede was matted with dried rain and the side on which it had been lying was dark and caked with earth. The discovery did not mean anything. It was not a clue. It only showed what degree of thoroughness he could expect of the black-haired man's investigations. The shoe could have been flung there when she was thrown clear or kicked there later. It only showed that he was a fool to come here because nothing he could find after this time would mean anything, except a socket wrench, and he had seen the truck-driver take that with him.

Sand Point, Janice had said, after she had been there long enough to get tired of it, was out at the end of nowhere, and why any person would deliberately choose to live in a place where you had to go a quarter of a mile to the mailbox and five miles to the nearest store, and then you didn't have anything except the store and gasoline pump and a sign saying Rio Vista; why any civilized human being would deliberately exile himself or herself to a forgotten corner of the woods like that, she couldn't understand. Even if the view was good, she couldn't understand it. Views were all right, but they were like movie stars: you liked them to look at, but to live with? Nix.

"You can let me out at the mailbox," Phillips said.

"Don't be silly," the girl said. "You can't walk that road with your leg, and I've got to turn the car around, anyway."

It had been different when they first came there, and as they drove up he remembered the way she had looked, seeing it for the first time through the trees. *Why, it's a log cabin,* she had said a little uncertainly; and then she had seen the wide expanse of the bay glittering beyond with early morning sunshine. She jumped out when they stopped and ran to the edge of the bluff, heedless of the fact that the grass had not been cut that year and was wet with dew. *Baby, it's gorgeous!* she cried, and whirled to kiss him. That was before she snagged her last pair of nylons where the bark was flaking off the logs by the front door, and found a mouse in the bathtub, and decided that views and fresh air could come too high. . . .

"It's a lovely place, Mr. Phillips," the girl said as she stopped the car in the circle off the garage, also built of logs.

"My folks like it," he said. She glanced at him, and he laughed. "I mean, it seems a little far-fetched to leave the bark on the logs and then do the inside in knotty pine with hardwood floors. . . . Do you want to see it?" Suddenly he found himself unable to walk into the place alone.

"Oh, no," she said. "You must be tired and Dad will be wondering where I've got to with the car."

"Yes," he said. "Of course. Thanks an awful lot for the lift. . . ."

He tried to make his voice sound right but he could feel the house waiting behind him, empty.

The girl smiled quickly. "All right," she said, "just for a minute."

When she left she said she was living with her father at

the Brown place on Polling Creek; you turned left at the filling station and it was the last house on the road, and they would love to have him drop around some time. He watched the car drive away. Then he went back into the house to get something to eat. There was a small gold wristwatch lying on top of the refrigerator where Janice had placed it for safety before doing the dishes after lunch that day. He closed the refrigerator door very carefully and went back into the room he had been using as a study and lay down on the studio couch. Janice's picture looked at him smilingly from its frame on his desk. He lay there telling himself that he was not going to get up and put it out of sight, but he did.

IV

Shaving, he had explained to Janice, was something a man liked to do the same way every time. He preferred, he had said, to keep the brush on the right-hand side of the medicine cabinet and the bowl on the left-hand side. If she insisted, he would keep the bowl to the right and the brush to the left. He did not, however, he had informed her, take kindly to the idea of finding them now one way and now the other. *But what earthly difference can it make, baby? she had protested. It isn't as if you used them up there. You always have to take them down, anyway, don't you?*

He opened the window beside him and looked out. Outside, the early morning sun was gradually taking the dampness out of the air and shortening the shadows under the trees. The bay was quite calm, what he could see of it, and a little smoky with mist. He felt a great deal better than he had the day before. He had slept all afternoon, grabbed a bottle of beer and a sandwich, and slept all night, dreamlessly; a fact that rather disturbed him. It seemed a little disloyal to be able to sleep like that.

He looked at the brush in his hand. In spite of what she had said, she had never put it back wrong since the day he mentioned it; she would remember something like that when you least expected her to. But it had been wrong this morning. He lathered his chin and began to shave. The coffee began to bubble in the Silex in the kitchen and he ran out to rescue it. Standing there in his pajama trousers with the razor in his hand he took careful stock of the kitchen, and the bread-knife was in the knife-rack where it should have belonged and didn't; and the extra paring knife they kept in the rack in the bread-knife slot, because it was sharp, was in the open table drawer where they usually kept the bread-knife. And yet, a hundred and twenty dollar gold watch lay untouched on top of the refrigerator, as if to give the lie to the idea that somebody had been through the house.

He went back to the bathroom and finished shaving. When he reached for a pair of slacks in the closet, they were hanging on a wooden hanger, while his good sports coat hung on a metal wire article. He always kept the coat on the wooden hanger to keep the shoulders from breaking down. He dressed and went into the kitchen and fried himself a pair of eggs sunnyside up while the toast was making. He thought the salt and pepper shakers above the stove were reversed, but he could not be sure. He was reasonably certain that the allspice had been at the right end of the shelf. He remembered the torn label. The allspice was now in the middle.

He ate hungrily and had a cigarette before doing the dishes.

It was, of course, possible that his mother had decided to clean house while he was in the hospital. She had come here for his clothes, and she had tidied the bedroom, which Janice had left, as usual, in a mess, after dressing for the party. His mother could have decided to do a job on the whole house, but it was not likely.

It was even possible that Jack and Vivian Cunningham had had a brainwave: *Poor Hugh in the hospital, we'd better see that everything's shipshape before he gets home.* One or two items might have been explained by the Brandons from up the shore coming by while he was gone to make sure nothing was running or burning or being rained on; or the Hartshornes from the other side; or Chris Wells might have dropped in. In fact, when you thought of the number of people who quite innocently could have entered Sand Point while he was away, the place took on the aspects of Grand Central Station.

But the chances of any of these people embarking on a program so ambitious as to result in this wholesale juggling of small and relatively inaccessible items was, he had to admit, very slight. Every time he reached for something it was somewhere else. The dish towel had fallen behind the sink, the scouring powder was hidden behind the soap flakes, and he could not find the steel wool to clean up the frying pan. Somebody had been through the house, leaving an expensive watch on the refrigerator, refusing to soil their hands with a couple of hundred dollars' worth of silver flatware, and even turning up their nose at thirty dollars in cash that he had left tucked under an ashtray on the dresser in his study.

Nothing in the house was as Janice had left it, and it was as if the unknown, by moving everything just a little, had drawn a veil over the part of the life that she had shared.

"But why?" he asked aloud. "What the hell would they want?"

He dried his hands on the dish towel, took the cigarette from his mouth and extinguished it under the tap, threw it in the garbage can, and walked slowly out of the kitchen to the door of the bedroom; then he stopped, for a moment unable to make himself go inside. . . . He would go inside and say that breakfast would be ready in a few minutes and she would sit up drowsily in the big bed, not quite awake, having fallen asleep again after he left the room. He would throw her bathing suit at her and pull on his trunks, and they would run out of the house and down the steep steps to the dock and dive in. If it was very early and nobody around they sometimes neglected the bathing suits.

Then they would dry themselves and go to breakfast in their bathrobes. . . .

He shivered a little and opened the door, and the bed was, of course, smooth and empty under the yellow chenille spread. He went to the dresser and found her gold cigarette case untouched among the loose jewelry carelessly heaped in the top drawer. It was of no use to check through the jewelry because he had only a vague notion of what should be there. It was all new, anyway. The cigarette case she had owned when he first met her. He turned it over in his hands. It was engraved with the initials *J.G.*, for Janice Gray. He had always been quite sure that a man had given it to her because it was so much more expensive than anything else she had brought with her.

He opened it and found three cigarettes. On the inside edge, in fine engraving, was the name of the maker: *Huntsman, Los Angeles.* She had never told him if his hypothesis were correct; sometimes when he kidded her about it she would seem to admit it, other times she would get angry, but usually she would merely laugh. *If you really want me to,* she had said once, *I'll throw it away,* making as if to pitch it through the car window. He had seized her wrist and she had laughed at him. *Well, make up your mind, baby. I don't want to keep it if it makes you unhappy.*

He found himself wishing the unknown had taken the case with him, but it was still there, in his hands, unwanted: like the white slipper he had found on the hillside it was not a clue. It did not mean anything. It was merely something she had owned for a while and did not need any more.

He put the case gently down on the dresser and turned and walked out of the room. Suddenly it was more important to get her belongings packed up, ready to be taken away, so that the house would, at least, be free of the things she had worn, played in, slept in, abused, and treasured, than it was to discover what, if anything, the unknown had wanted. But when he had the trunk and the two suitcases up from the cellar, and an armful of her dresses off the hangers, he found that he could not go through with it. Even with Janice dead, you could not throw her dresses in a heap in the corner of a trunk. They would have to be packed as she would have packed them, and he could not stand to do it; he would have to ask his mother to do it.

He dropped the load on the bed, smoothing it a little so it would not look too untidy, and turned to the dresser drawers. These were untidy already, and he could make himself take the things out by the double handful; and when he reached the bottom drawer a small roll of paper fell to the floor and disappeared under the bed.

He stood for a moment looking after it uncertainly, his hands buried in the silk of the peach-colored slip in which it had been wrapped. Then he let the bright cloth fall back into the drawer and kneeled beside the bed. The paper was stiff to his fingers and he knew what it was before he had it in sight: a photograph rolled into a cylinder and tied with a string. He found himself trembling a little as he straightened up; and, before slipping off the string, he pushed the dresses aside and sat down on the bed. Then he rolled the string off the end of the cylinder and spread the picture out flat on his knee and sat looking at it.

In the picture she was singing. She wore an evening gown of black satin and her dark hair was loose about her white shoulders. From somewhere outside the picture a spotlight struck highlights from her hair and lips, and from the shining black dress; and there was an orchestra behind her. She had her hands a little outstretched in a gesture of renunciation, and she was singing her heart out to an invisible audience, and he could hear the song quite plainly. It had love in it, and heartbreak, and promise; and every man listening would know that the promise was for him.

He looked at the picture very carefully, but there was no doubt at all that the girl was Janice.

When he let it go, the picture coiled itself shut like a spring and rolled off his knee to the floor. He looked at it but made no effort to reach it. He could still hear her singing and it was unbearable that she was dead. . . .

After a little he got up and blew his nose and hung all the dresses back in the closet and closed the suitcases and the drawers on their jumbled contents. Then he took the photograph with him out into the living room, closing the door behind him. He could feel a steady throbbing in his head and he went into the bathroom and took three aspirin tablets, with water, and made himself a drink, and returned to the living room.

Once, a few weeks ago, when they were dancing to the phonograph at the Hartshornes' next door, Janice slipped out of his arms as they passed the instrument and leaned over it, listening, her toe beating time to the music. She was just a little drunk. Then she began to sing as if there were nobody in the room but the two of them. Everybody there, Chris Wells and Frank Hartshorne, the Cunninghams, and some people from up the shore, gradually stopped dancing to listen. When Janice became aware of them all watching her she hesitated, laughed, and finished the lyrics in a wild burlesque. Then, while they were clapping, she curtseyed and ran out on the porch. When he reached her, she was crying. *Take me home, baby, I'm tight,* she gasped, burying her face in his shoulder.

He let the picture roll itself up at last. The stamp on the back read: *Paul Linz, Hollywood.* There seemed to be no reason to doubt its authenticity, or the authenticity of the photograph. At some time Janice had sung with a band, probably on the West Coast. Yet he had found her inexpertly pounding a typewriter at Johns Hopkins University, on the other side of the continent. Even if she had failed to make good in the long run it did not explain why she should want to keep the episode a secret; and she had kept it a secret deliberately. He had commented on her singing often enough, so that it would have been simple and easy for her to show him the picture and tell him about it, but the most she had ever said was that she had had a few lessons when she was a kid.

There were three things about the picture that were significant, he reflected as, rising, he went into the study and put it away with the other picture he had of her: Janice had kept it, therefore it had been important to her; she had never told him about it, therefore it represented a part of her life of which she had been ashamed or afraid; and, finally, the unknown had not wanted it. Therefore it was not the reason why the house had been searched.

But perhaps it was. He dismissed the idea that a man who would examine the medicine chest and the knife-rack in the kitchen would miss an eight-by-ten photograph simply because it was wrapped in a peach-colored silk slip; but if the man's name were Holt . . . If the black-haired man from the sheriff's office had searched the house to discover why Hugh Phillips should want to claim that his wife had been murdered, he would not have wanted to remove anything. It would have been simple enough for him to have the picture copied and returned in plenty of time. He would not want anything to be missing when Hugh Phillips came back, because it was unlikely that he had bothered to provide himself with a warrant.

The black-haired man had searched the house. Janice had sung in a band and suffered some experience painful enough to make her want to leave that life behind forever. The truck-driver had killed Janice in a fit of panic. It was all very pretty and it did not make sense. There was no relation between the items except that they all revolved about the life of one girl, who was dead. One would prefer the world to be a little more logical, but perhaps it wasn't.

V

In the afternoon he went down to the pier and found that, as he had expected, the sailboat was badly in need of bailing after a week's neglect. Three seasons of disuse while he was away had not done it any good, and in spite of the work he had done on it that spring it still leaked. It was seventeen feet long, sloop rigged, and the name *Starlight* was stenciled in gold on the mahogany transom.

The boat had not been used very much that summer. Janice had not thought much of sailing; she had not liked the boat's tendency to deviate from the horizontal as the wind increased, and she had taken a dim view of getting her fanny wet. Sailing, she had said, was like horseback riding; as a sport it was all right for those who liked it, but as a means of transportation it stank.

He did not like to remember the ways in which they had disagreed; it seemed, now that she was dead, like a form of betrayal. He stood looking down at the two rowboats, also partially full of water. They did not matter, but if the sailboat filled beyond a certain point the weight of the tall mast capsized it and righting it again was a mess. He was sitting on the green canvas deck, bailing left-handed to keep the water away from his bandaged leg, when Christine Wells's convertible drove up beside the garage on the bluff above him.

He stopped bailing and watched Chris come down the long flight of wooden stairs. She was wearing a white tennis suit, and the pleated shorts flared a little with each downward step she took. Even at a distance she looked freshly laundered and clean and sunburned; a moderately tall, athletic girl with long light hair, tied back at the nape of her neck with a pink ribbon, so that it looked a little old fashioned.

With her complexion, she doesn't need to be beautiful, Janice had said the first time she saw Chris. Another time he had been a little surprised to find the two of them chatting pleasantly in the living room at Sand Point. *Oh, I think she's nice,* Janice had said later, with one of her murderous little pauses, *in a bovine sort of way.* He had pointed out, vaguely nettled, that Chris could probably have worn any of Janice's dresses. Surprisingly, Janice had refused to lose her temper. *Yes, and wouldn't she look like a damn fool,* Janice had said, smiling. *I wasn't talking about her figure, stupid.*

It made him feel curiously happy, in a guilty sort of

way, to watch Chris come along the dock toward him; but there was a small, uncomfortable pause when she reached him. She steadied him as, jumping to the dock, he let his weight come on the injured leg.

"Ouch," he said. "Thanks."

"Don't fall in," she said.

They studied each other warily, as if they had not seen each other for a long time. He noticed that her light hair, as always in summer, had turned blonde in streaks from the sun. It seemed a funny thing to be noticing in August, when he had been seeing her around almost continuously for two months. Her skin had a golden color from the sun, very different from Janice's dusky tan; and she wore no make-up except lipstick.

She said, "Mother thought you might want to come over for dinner."

"Sure," he said. "Thanks." He turned away to make the sailboat fast. "You didn't come to see me in the hospital," he said lightly, but without looking at her. "All I got was a mess of ghoulish sympathy from Jack and Vivian."

She hesitated. "I couldn't, Hugh," she said soberly. "You know what I mean."

He knew that she was thinking of what Janice had said to her that night.

"I know," he said. "I was just kidding."

"Are you all right now?"

"Sure," he said. "Healthy as a pup."

She looked at him for a moment; and they were both, he knew, trying to find some natural way of bringing Janice into the conversation, so that they could dispose of her casually; then Chris turned away.

They climbed slowly to the top of the bluff. Below them the dock and the boats and the river were in sunshine; and beyond the mouth of the river, the bay was bright and clear to the low dark line of the Eastern Shore, but at the top of the bluff the trees cast a heavy shadow. He glanced at the house and it seemed to stare back at him, silently accusing, because he was going off with Christine Wells. He got into the convertible beside her.

She always drove a convertible, usually with the top down; and always with a slightly apologetic air, as if afraid that someone might think she was being flashy or ostentatious. He could feel her silence as she turned the car around and headed down the drive toward the sunshine beyond the trees.

"What are you going to do now?" she asked at last.

"I think I'll stick it out here till the fall term," he said. "Then maybe I'll move in with the folks. I don't know."

"Jack and Vivian seemed to think you'd move in right away." Her voice was a little surprised that he would want to stay on.

He said, "I've got to get used to the idea, Chris."

"Did you love her very much?"

He glanced at her quickly, startled and shocked that she would ask such a question. "That's a hell of a thing to ask," he said. "I married her, didn't I? Right now . . . right now I feel like a man who's lost his leg; it may not have been the best damn leg in the world, but it was his leg and he misses it like hell. Does that answer your question?"

He did not hear her reply. It was occurring to him coldly that he did not really know Christine Wells any longer. He did not know with whom she had been going, or, except sketchily, what she had been doing, or what kind of person she had turned out to be. They had never really become reacquainted with each other after the war. Since his marriage to Janice he had seen her around, and talked to her, and danced with her at various people's houses; and there had never, even at the first, been any particular constraint between them; but neither had there, of course, been any particular intimacy, no matter what Janice had claimed that night. They had simply acted like two people who had known each other for years.

He had never allowed himself to dwell on what Chris's feelings might have been the afternoon he called her long distance to tell her he was marrying Janice. When you did something quite unforgivable, it was better simply not to think about it.

When he returned from the Pacific she had been working in New York. They had decided, sensibly, that since he was going to be very busy at the University, she might as well continue working until the fall, particularly since the people had been very nice to her and were now asking her, as a favor, to stay on two months longer. They had waited so long, they had agreed, that it would be a little silly to start rushing things now. In the fall they could get married the way people should get married. . . . He remembered her remote voice in the telephone, saying *It's all right, Hugh. It was nice of you to call me. I'm glad you called. Good luck. . . .*

"There's Mother," Chris said.

He looked up with a guilty start to see Mrs. Wells come to the door to greet them as they drove up. He glanced quickly at the girl beside him, but he could not tell if she, too, had been remembering what had happened a year ago.

Sand Point looked dark and deserted when they returned. He heard the frogs croaking in the ravine below the house, and the fireflies were out. *Honey, come quick,* Janice had shouted, *it's Fourth of July out here.* She had never seen fireflies before, and he had caught half a dozen in a mason jar so that she could watch them flashing.

"Thanks a lot," he said, opening the car door. "I was getting pretty tired of my own cooking."

Christ waited behind the wheel while he climbed out. "If you need anything in town . . ."

"I'll let you know. Thanks." He glanced at her. Nothing was the way it had been, nor would it ever be that way again, but he asked, "Do you want to come in for a moment, Chris?"

She hesitated. "All right, but I'd better be getting home soon." She smiled. "I have a date."

"Anybody I know?"

"Frank. Frank Hartshorne."

There was nothing wrong with Frank Hartshorne, whose folks owned the big white house up the river. Frank was all right and there was nothing to be annoyed about. He had no right to be annoyed. But he was realizing that he had counted, vaguely, on Christine Wells from the minute he first realized that Janice was dead; never allowing the thought to come to the surface of his mind, because it would have seemed disloyal, but feeling it there, solid and reassuring: when everything was settled and smoothed away, Chris would be there. It was a particularly arrogant masculine idea to have had, he realized. Chris owed him no consideration at all. It was very generous of her to have thought of having him over for dinner. When you came right down to it, all Chris owed him was a kick in the face.

Her white shorts and shirt made a sharp pattern in front of him as they came into the living room. He turned on the light.

"Drink?"

"Just a Coke," she said.

"With rum in it?"

She shook her head. He splashed a jigger of rum into a glass from the sideboard, left the second glass plain, and finished the job in the kitchen. When he returned, she was reclining in a deep chair with her long tanned legs stretched out in front of her, crossed at the ankles.

"Nice," he said.

"Not as nice as hers."

"You've got the tact of a hippopotamus today," he said irritably.

She looked up at him, smiling a little, and took the glass from his hand. "I'm a very tactful girl," she said calmly. "But when two people have been throwing things at each other for almost a year and then one dies and the other goes into a heartbreak routine that would panic Broadway, I find it a little silly, Hugh."

He stood watching her face, too surprised to speak. She was still smiling at him, but he saw that there were fine lines of strain around her eyes, as if she were smiling into a bright light.

"She told me all about it, you see. If I'd asked, she'd probably have shown me the bruises."

He turned away and walked carefully to the chair by the radio and sat down. There was no doubt in his mind

119

as to the incident to which she was referring; but he could not quite accept the fact that Janice had told anybody, particularly Chris.

"She heaved an ashtray at me," he said. "So I turned her over and warmed her bottom."

He had asked Janice politely to turn the radio down a little, and she had turned it up instead, so he came out of the study and jerked the plug from the wall and she slapped him and he slapped her back and she threw an ashtray at him. It went through the big front window. He grabbed her and she struck at him with her nails. She was screaming at him. He had never been so angry in his life. They had been building up to it for weeks.

"But you can see," Chris said stiffly, "that it makes this bereaved husband act just a wee bit ridiculous." The smile on her face looked as if she had forgotten it there.

"She did have a habit of swinging at me occasionally," he admitted. "It didn't mean anything. After a while I just started swinging back."

When he had let her go, Janice had sat up in the middle of the floor, her dress twisted and her dark hair wild and the room a shambles about her. He had stood over her, feeling of the scratches on his face; and suddenly they had both burst out laughing; and he had picked her up and carried her out of the room. He could remember the way her arms had come around his neck, and the way she had kissed him, still laughing a little, as he kicked the door shut behind them.

But Chris thought that if you hit a person you must hate them. Chris had probably never even kicked a wastepaper basket across the room in a temper: she would have thought it showed a dreadful lack of self-control.

"I didn't know she went around boasting about it," he said slowly.

Chris smiled. "She told me a great many things about you, Hugh. I think she was lonely out here. And of course I'm not really stupid enough not to know why she picked me to confide in: after all, she knew we'd been engaged once."

He said carefully, "You didn't like her very much, did you, Chris?"

"I didn't dislike her," Chris said stiffly. "She was fun to talk to. But I don't suppose you can ever get very fond of a girl who's taken a man away from you, can you?" She smiled again, and he knew that she was trying to keep up an illusion that they were talking frankly and good-naturedly about something that did not really concern either of them. She put her glass on the arm of her chair, looking at him across the room. "I guess I'm really prejudiced by what she said that night, Hugh, and it isn't really fair, but . . . Not about you and me, because that was just silly, but . . . No girl likes to be told that she is 'untouched and untouchable,' " she murmured, turning pink and looking away.

"She was a little tight," Hugh Phillips said.

"I know," Chris said. Her smile faltered and died as she looked at him again. "I guess I'd better go, Hugh," she said helplessly. "I'm sorry. I don't know what made me . . ."

"She was murdered, Chris," he said.

He remembered that before the war he had occasionally wondered guiltily what Chris would do if one evening, instead of just kissing her nicely, he mauled her around a bit: the idea had seemed somehow indecent, like thinking of making a pass at your own sister. But there were times when you wanted to startle Chris, or shock her, just to see what would happen.

Suddenly it was intolerable that they should have been sitting calmly in the living room that had been Janice's, taking Janice apart in a kind of spiritual post-mortem: intolerable, and disloyal and cruel. He got sharply to his feet.

"She was murdered," he said. "A man beat her head in with a wrench, and I lay with my leg in a crack, watching. He hit her twice, just to make sure, and went up to the road and drove away. Even if she did slap my face occasionally, I don't think she had that coming to her. . . ."

"Don't, Hugh!"

He looked at Chris and finished his drink and turned

away from her to the sideboard. Then Chris was beside him, holding his wrist.

"I'll drink as much as I damn well please," he said, pulling free. "If you want to be helpful, get a Coke out of the refrigerator. You know where it is."

She went and came back with the bottle and he emptied it into the glass on top of the rum. He found himself grinning wryly.

"Damn if I'm not putting on an act," he said. Chris did not smile, but watched him. She never tanned so deeply that you could not see the color change in her face; and he could see that she was quite pale. He tried to make her smile: "I'm an unstable personality. You shouldn't have anything to do with me. . . . Oh, for Pete's sake!" he exploded. "She was! I'm not trying to kid you. Don't *you* go telling me what I saw."

"I don't understand," Chris whispered. "Why didn't you tell . . ."

"I let them talk me out of it," he said. "Some local politician didn't want to be bothered. I let him talk me out of it. He almost had me believing it was a hallucination. Most persuasive sort of chap, in a Gestapo sort of way. He threatened me with everything from manslaughter to first-degree murder, besides telling me it wouldn't do any good."

"But," Chris said, "there was an inquest, wasn't there, Hugh?"

He looked at her and realized that she did not believe him. He could see that she did not know what to believe, and that it frightened her. He remembered suddenly what the black-haired man had said about murder. *Nobody wants to have anything to do with murder,* Mr. Holt had said, and apparently he was right.

"Skip it," he said. "Just skip the whole thing."

He turned and walked to the fireplace and stood looking down at it. The last time they had had a fire was some six weeks ago, but the half-burned logs still lay untidily on the andirons. Some lipstick-stained cigarette butts lay among the ashes where Janice had thrown them carelessly some time when there had been no ashtray handy. You tried to remember things the way you would have liked them to be but there was always something or somebody to remind you of the way they had actually been. He heard Chris come up behind him.

"It wouldn't have done any good," he said without turning around. "Don't you see, Chris, it wouldn't have done any good, because if they didn't want to find the evidence, they just wouldn't find it. You can't buck a set-up like that. I ought to know. I'm supposed to have a degree in sociology. And there would have been a big mess in the papers about her. . . ." He turned and saw Chris's eyes watching him steadily enough, but there was fear in them.

"But why, Hugh, why?"

"He just got rattled. He'd left his truck there in the way, don't you see, and she was yelling at him. . . ."

"I mean . . ." Chris licked her lips. ". . . why didn't the man want you to . . . ?"

He shrugged. "I don't know. I know it sounds screwy. . . . All right," he said. "You don't believe me." She did not say anything. Presently he went on, "The guy *said* he thought I'd been seeing things. He *said* I'd had a bad crack on the head and didn't really know what had happened."

Her face seemed to light up with intense relief. He saw everything become clear to her. He had been delirious and the nice man had calmed him down. There really had been no murder. It was just something he had dreamed; and she of course was not asking herself why he should have dreamed it.

"Don't say it, Chris," Hugh Phillips said. "I don't want to hear you say it."

She was a very nice girl, Christine Wells, and she did not want to hurt anybody, and she was very sorry for him.

"If it did happen they'll find out all about it sooner or later, won't they?" she said reassuringly.

"Sure," he said. "Goodnight, Chris."

He stood on the porch watching the fireflies long after the tail-lights of the convertible had turned onto the main road. He walked slowly to the front of the porch and he did not want Christine Wells. He wanted to hear the radio and the husky voice singing snatches of song a little more loudly than was necessary; not really meaning to irritate him, but just reminding him that he had a wife, like a kid being just a little naughty to get attention.

He was glad he had refrained from telling Chris about the picture; although that was the reason he had asked her in, to show her the picture, and ask her if Janice had ever said anything that might explain it.

VI

In the morning when he woke he saw the gun lying on the lamp table beside the bed. In the evening it had seemed quite logical to get it up from the top shelf of the locker in the cellar where his father stored the guns and fishing tackle, because if there were really anything to the idea he had had in the hospital when he said he could identify Janice's murderer, then a gun might be a good thing to have around. But now in the morning, with sunlight in the room, the idea seemed far-fetched and ridiculous. Having the gun there looked as if he were afraid of the dark or of being alone in the house. He slipped the long-barreled .38 target revolver into a desk drawer to get it out of sight.

Jack and Vivian Cunningham arrived while he was making breakfast. They brought a large cardboard carton of groceries and said that if he needed anything else just to let them know. Hardly had they left when the Desters, in town, called to say that they were coming out to see the Brandons, and could they bring anything. It seemed that everybody had suddenly remembered that the Phillips boy (Dr. Phillips's son, you remember, his wife was killed in that dreadful accident last week) was out at Sand Point alone without a car.

The Black Cross

Old Mr. Hartshorne was driving up to Baltimore, and it would be no trouble at all to stop by the Phillipses' apartment if there was anything to be taken up, or did Hugh want to go himself? Mrs. Wells dropped by on her way to do her weekly shopping. Mr. French at the store in Rio Vista called that he was making a delivery to the Williamses up the road and could easily stop by on the way. He had some fine pork chops, Mr. French said. Mr. Saunders, the mailman, brought the mail clear up to the house, with last night's paper that had been in the box.

When the green Pontiac came up the drive, Phillips recognized it but could not remember to whom it belonged. A man was driving. Then a girl got out and stood in the drive a little irresolutely, looking toward the house. She had an abruptly upturned nose in a square, small, almost childish face; and her complexion was as clear as Christine Wells's. Her body was all legs. It was the girl who had driven the other car; who had given him a lift from the courthouse after the inquest. She was wearing a black peasant skirt that had a band of bright embroidery near the hem, and a wide white patent-leather belt that made her waist seem very small. Her thin, short-sleeved white blouse looked just right for high school.

She turned and told the man in the car to wait a minute, and came running across the lawn toward the house. Phillips liked the way she ran. Most girls ran cautiously and uneasily, as if they were put together with safety pins. He liked the way her short brown hair looked in the sunshine. He liked everything about her, in fact, except that he could not for the moment remember her name. Then it came to him: Shirley. Shirley Carlson. He went forward and opened the screen door.

"Oh, I was afraid you weren't . . ." Shirley Carlson caught her breath. "We were just driving into town and wondered if you'd . . ."

He could not help laughing.

"Did I say something?" the girl asked, flushing a little.

"No, it's swell of you, Miss Carlson," he said hastily. "Really, it's swell, it's just that everybody . . ."

She touched her hair and said, a little stiffly, "Yes, Dad

said your friends would probably be taking care of you all right. I just thought . . . Well, Dad's waiting in the car. . . ."

"Can't you come in for a drink? Both of you?"

"Oh, no, we've got to get to town before the banks close, Mr. Phillips." She retreated down the steps. He could see it occur to her that he might think she was embarrassed or annoyed at finding that she had made her father drive several miles out of the way on a fruitless errand. "Come down to the car, why don't you?" she asked, smiling quickly. "I'd like you to meet my father."

As he walked across the lawn beside her, he found himself thinking that even though his hands were not very large he could probably make them meet around her if she sucked in a little. He thought he would like to try it. A tall man in a gray summer worsted suit got out of the car as they approached.

"Dad, this is Mr. Phillips," the girl said, a little awkwardly.

The tall man shook hands and pushed at Shirley Carlson's hair. "I told the kid you'd be taken care of," he said, grinning, to Phillips. "But she was all bothered you were starving to death out here. . . ."

Hugh Phillips watched them drive off. There was no reason why he should not have gone with them, he realized; he could have manufactured some excuse. He frowned, irritated with himself for not thinking of this in time. Then, walking slowly back to the house, he grinned, remembering the way the girl had flushed and ducked into the car, very annoyed with her father. He remembered the address she had told him earlier: the Brown place on Polling Creek. If he were to go sailing later in the day or, say, tomorrow, there would, he reflected, be nothing against putting into Polling Creek, sort of by accident.

The mail and paper lay where he had put them on the living-room table. He took the paper across the room to the big chair by the radio. An editorial on the front page discussed the coming election for sheriff, but made no reference to a man named Holt.

The Black Cross

Hugh Phillips folded the paper carefully, wondering what would happen if he walked into the *Herald's* office on Main Street and told his story, with emphasis on the strange behavior of Mr. Holt; but it struck him coldly that until he had discovered more about the picture, and Janice's reasons for concealing it and the part of her life it represented, he was not in a position to demand publicity for the manner of her death.

He walked to the table and sorted the mail through his hands, and read a letter from his mother asking how he was feeling and did he want her to come down. She was, his mother wrote, a little worried about his being down there all alone without a car. . . .

The house was very quiet. Outside there was sunshine and the steady bright chirping of the crickets; but the house only seemed darker and more silent by contrast. A car approached along the main road but did not turn in.

There were so many things unexplained, he thought; there was the black-haired man and the truck-driver, and there was the small nagging question in Hugh Phillips's mind of how a wound inflicted in the manner and with the weapon he had seen could have passed the doctor as the normal result of an automobile accident. (You knew what you had seen, but after a while the images became blurred with being looked at so often and so hard, and you began to wonder a little if you had really seen them like that.) There was the fact that the house had been searched, and that came back to the black-haired man, and to the picture he had not taken, or, if taken, returned. But always you came back to the triangle of the black-haired man, the picture, and the fact of murder. You came back to Janice, who had been murdered.

There was Janice and her picture and her cigarette case; and there was what he had never questioned before, the money she had had to spend. *I've got a couple of thousand in the bank in case we need it, honey,* she had told him before they were married. It had seemed to him a large sum for her circumstances and salary, and he had said so. She had answered, laughing, that she had had a

127

long time to save it in, and he had never brought the subject of her money up again, because it embarrassed him a little. Once, later, he had protested mildly that a hundred and eighty dollar evening gown was hardly practical, considering the number of times they went out, and the kind of places they went to. *But darling, what's the use of having money if you don't spend it?* she had asked, and there had been a slight edge to her voice that told him to leave it alone. It was her money, as the car was her car. He had looked forward to the time when it would be gone, a little uneasily, wondering how she would adjust herself to the reality of his limited income.

He put down his mother's letter and walked quickly into the bedroom. The room was very still and, with the windows closed, rather warm and stuffy, although the sun was off the drawn blinds. He groped among the jewelry and gloves and handkerchiefs in the top dresser drawer, knowing now what he was looking for, but Janice's bank book was not there; neither was it in any of her purses. The middle drawer of the dresser was empty; he had put the contents into a suitcase the day before. The lower drawer was half full as he had left it after discovering the picture. He found the bank book at the rear, and as he freed it from something black and very sheer that clung to his fingers like cobwebs and reminded him sharply and poignantly of Janice, he knew that he was frightened.

For most of the past six months, ever since she had started buying things, the little book in its dog-eared envelope had lain in the drawer with her jewelry, when it was not on top of the dresser, or on the mantelpiece, or in some other conspicuous place where she had put it to remind herself not to forget it. There had never been any secret about it. If he had wanted to examine it, he had had a thousand chances. But shortly before her death she had apparently begun to hide it, as if there were now something in it that he should not see. . . . He discarded the envelope and opened the book.

She had started the account a couple of years before, in the fall, with a single entry of thirty-three hundred dollars; early the next spring she had withdrawn eight hundred, presumably for the car. Then in September of the same year she had withdrawn four hundred, and he knew that this had been spent for her trousseau. Five months had passed without change; they were married now, living in the little apartment in Baltimore. Right after Christmas she had seen a fur coat she liked, and that had been the beginning. At the bottom of the page there were only a hundred and twenty dollars left in the account.

He turned the page: on the fifteenth of May she had withdrawn the rest. They were moving to Sand Point and she needed clothes for the country. She had left one dollar to hold the account open. A little more than two months later, on the twenty-second of July, she had made a single deposit, the last entry in the book, of five thousand dollars.

July 22 —— 5000.00

There was a faint, rather stale smell of face powder and cologne in the room. He found himself taking the stopper out of one of the little cut-glass bottles on the glass-topped dresser; replacing it quickly when he realized what he was doing, but the rich sweet odor of her perfume seemed to burst into the room; and he went out quickly, closing the door behind him. He had a headache again. He took aspirin for it and went into the study and sat down on the studio couch.

July 22 —— 5000.00

Not fifty, or five hundred, or even a thousand—that she could conceivably have borrowed on something they owned—but five thousand. Even his parents could not readily have raised such a sum; and if they had given it to her, whatever her pretext for wanting it, he would have known something was wrong from their attitude, even if she had sworn them to secrecy. And if she had got it from an account in another bank, or from war bonds, why had she hidden the little book after making the deposit?

July 22 —— 5000.00

He sat looking at the preposterous figure, almost twice his yearly salary, facing the slow reluctant knowledge that her money had, after all, run out, but it had not changed anything. She had not faced the reality of living on what he had had to offer her: it had not been enough. She had merely got more, somewhere.

Somewhere.

VII

Chris's voice over the telephone sounded concerned and a little puzzled.

"Is anything wrong, Hugh? Your leg . . . ?"

"No, I'm fine," he said. "I just want to talk to you. If you're busy, skip it."

He knew two things instinctively: that she did not want to come and that there was someone with her.

"Never mind," he said as she hesitated. "It wasn't important."

"Don't be silly," she said. "I'll be right over."

He put down the receiver gently and made himself a drink, trying not to admit to himself that, in spite of everything else he had to think about, it hurt to know that Chris did not want to see him. Of course she was right. You could not go back a year and start over again; and you could not really play comfortably at being friends with a girl whom you had left, so to speak, waiting at the church. There was nothing in it for either of them any more. But she was the only person his own age that he could consider discussing Janice with; and she had been the only person Janice had talked to; and he had already told her part of the story.

She drove up in Frank Hartshorne's car, as if to answer his question of who her company had been. The big maroon coupé turned in the drive and headed out; and Chris came up to the porch.

"Mother took the car to town," she said. "Frank drove me over."

"He could have stuck around for a drink," Phillips said.

Chris smiled, and he knew that the smile was for both of them: herself for finding it necessary to explain why Frank had brought her, and Hugh Phillips for pretending he had wanted the other man to stay.

She was wearing the same, or another, white playsuit with a skirt belted over the pleated shorts but not buttoned down the front. Her hair was loose today, held back from her face by a wide black velvet band; but the trouble with Chris Wells was that she was too tall to look cute. She was too conservative to look truly smart, and she was too nice to look sexy. She looked fine on the beach, but the more clothes she put on the more she looked like just a nice wholesome girl that you would be delighted to have your best friend going around with.

This manner of thinking, he realized abruptly, was brought on by jealousy because she had not wanted to come and had arrived with Frank Hartshorne.

"Well. . . ." Chris said a little uncertainly.

"Come on in," he said. He could feel the drink he had just finished and, looking at his watch, he saw with surprise that it read five minutes of three; and he had not eaten lunch. "How about the kitchen?" he asked. "I haven't had lunch yet."

In the kitchen she helped him build a sandwich and gave herself a glass of milk. They sat down at the table. The refrigerator made a small whirring noise in the corner, and water dripped uneasily in the sink from a leaky faucet that he had never got around to fixing.

"What did you want to talk about, Hugh?" Chris asked. There was a slight impatience in her voice, as if being with him made her uncomfortable, and she would like to get away quickly.

"About Janice," he said. "You said she used to talk to you."

Chris hesitated. "Yes."

He glanced at her, surprised by her hesitation, and saw that her eyes were suddenly watching him, too steadily. You would look at a person like that if you knew something about them that you did not want to have to talk about. He looked away.

"Did she . . ." he said carefully, ". . . did she ever tell you about singing with a band?"

"Yes, Hugh."

He sat very still and did not look up from his sandwich, waiting for her to go on, but she did not go on. He took a deep bite of the sandwich, holding it away from him so that the mayonnaise would drip back to the plate instead of onto his slacks. This was Christine Wells, he told himself, Chris Wells whom he had known all his life, and why did they have to play games with each other? Even if he had not been very nice to her a year ago.

"Did she tell you why she quit?" he asked, without looking up.

"Yes."

"Can't you say anything but yes, Chris?"

"What do you want me to say?"

"You might," he said, "tell me about it."

"You don't know?"

He looked up, startled by something in her voice. "How the hell would I know?" he demanded. "If I knew would I be asking you? Do you think I'm talking for the fun of it?"

Chris said gently, "I didn't realize you were asking, Hugh. I thought you wanted to tell me something."

He glanced at her irritably and went to the sink to wash his hands. The faucet continued to drip, no matter how firmly he closed it. He came back to the table and she was still sitting there watching him, not having moved. He looked down at her and saw that she was holding herself very tightly against something; but whether against fear or anger or merely distaste for the conversation, he could not tell. Once he would have been able to tell, but he did not know her that well any longer.

"Tell you what?" he asked. Something moved in her eyes as she looked at him, and he knew that it was fear. He tried to ignore it, because it did not make sense. "Come on into the study, Chris," he said. "I'll show you what I found."

He had forgotten about the gun. When he pulled the drawer open he heard her gasp to see the large blued-steel weapon lying there beside the pictures. He took it out deliberately and laid it on the desk. She had seen it before, she had shot it herself, so why, he asked himself irritably, should the damn thing frighten her now? He pulled out the studio photograph he had put away the first night, when he could not stand to look at it, and replaced it where it had been on the desk, setting it up on its easel. Then he drew the rolled print out and closed the drawer and turned.

"This is all I know, Chris," he said, holding it out. "This and her bank book. I found the picture yesterday."

She glanced at him and took the picture, and he watched her slip the string off and stretch it flat between her hands. She looked up, her eyes studying the soft, smiling studio photograph on the desk, comparing.

"She was . . . very beautiful, Hugh."

"Sure," he said. "Mona Lisa with a permanent wave. Sure. It's her, isn't it? I mean, you don't really have to look at the other picture to tell, do you? What are you stalling for, Chris?"

"I'm not. . . ."

"What's the matter with you, anyway? You're acting as if . . ." Something about the way she stood there, almost as if she were afraid of him, made the room seem to close in about him. He could feel his head throbbing, and he wished he could take time out for another aspirin. "Just tell me about it in your own words," he said savagely. "What *did* she tell you, anyway?"

Chris licked her lips and watched the photograph roll itself up in her hand. Then she spoke without looking away from it.

"She didn't really tell me, Hugh. You see, I recognized her. That night at the Hartshornes' when she sang. You remember. She ran out right afterward and made you take her home, because she knew I had recognized her and didn't want me to talk about it in front of you. The next day she came over and made me promise not to tell you. I wouldn't have, anyway. It wasn't . . . any of my business."

"Go on," he said. He took the photograph out of her hand and put it on the desk.

"Dad took us to the place," Chris said. "You remember, I wrote you when Mother and I went out to be with him while the *Asheville* was in dry-dock in San Pedro."

He nodded.

"Well," she went on, "we went to this place in Hollywood, and she was singing there. It was called the Grotto. When I met her the first time after . . . after you were married, I was sure I had seen her somewhere, but I couldn't remember, and after a while I forgot about it. Until she sang that night. I was shocked, I guess, and I kept staring at her to make sure, and she saw me and knew I had recognized her. So the next day she came over . . ."

". . . and made you promise not to tell," he finished. "You've said that once."

"Yes," Chris said with a small laugh. "I guess I have."

"Well," he said, "what's so terrible about that? She sang in a nightclub, so what? What's all the mystery about?"

Chris hesitated. "Don't you really know?"

"No," he said sharply. "I don't know."

"She was living with the man, Hugh."

He drew a deep breath. "All right," he said after a while. "All right. Lots of women do it, I've heard." He heard his own voice saying distantly, "What man?"

He did not hear her answer, as he turned away and started to sit down on the bright Navaho blanket that covered the studio couch, the pattern shifting geometrically in front of his eyes; then he saw the smiling picture watching him from the desk and he straightened up very quickly, and walked out of the room. There seemed to be a glare of light in the hallway, shot through with darting black specks, and he felt quite cold, but there was perspiration on his forehead. He stood there, feeling the ache in his head. *I must have hit it harder than the doctors gave me credit for,* he thought, lifting his hand clumsily to feel

134

the adhesive tape that still covered the bruise. Then Chris was beside him, steadying him and leading him to a chair in the living room.

"I'm all right," he said.

"I'll get you a drink."

"To hell with the drink," he said. Sitting with his head far back, he watched the room become clear; it was like watching the wind disperse a mist on the river. "Tell me," he said.

"They shouldn't have let you out of the hospital," Chris said. "You're not well, Hugh."

"I'm fine," he said. "I'm gorgeous. Sit down and stop stalling and tell me about it."

She sat down on the arm of his chair, looking at the fireplace across the room.

"How much do you know, Hugh?"

"I know what's in the picture," he said impatiently. She would insist that he knew something. "I know that she had three thousand in the bank right after she got to Baltimore, and a gold cigarette case with her initials on it. . . . What was her real name?"

"Gordon. Jane Gordon."

The strange name seemed to wipe out a year of his life. Janice Gray had never really existed. This, he realized, was quite true.

"I know," he said, "that about three weeks ago, after having cleaned out her savings account this spring, she rejuvenated it with the juicy sum of five thousand bucks."

He saw Chris start and look down at him, and felt a savage satisfaction at having told her something, for a change. Yet in some peculiar way her reaction brought her a little closer to him. They were both, at least, people to whom five thousand dollars was a great deal of money. He could see that the fear was back in Chris's eyes. She took the little book that he produced from his shirt pocket, but for a moment she was not looking at it, but at him.

"Listen," he said angrily, "have I got a wart on my nose, or what?"

She looked away and laughed. "No, of course not, why?"

Then she was studying the bank book. "Five thousand," she said quickly. "That's an awful lot of money, Hugh. Where could she . . . ?"

"I don't know," he said. He moved his tongue around his lips, forcing himself to go on: "This man . . . this man that Janice used to live with . . ."

"His name was Karl Lewis. He owned the Grotto."

"And how did you know she was . . . ?"

"It was in the papers," Chris said. "After the mur—"
She sat quite still. He had the impression that she had stopped breathing.

"Take it easy," he murmured. "Take it easy, Chris."

He got up and went to the sideboard. His hands, making the drinks, were quite steady. He went into the kitchen for ice and came back, and Chris was standing by the chair, watching him. He found himself wishing she would stop watching him so carefully.

He put a glass in her hand. "You'd got as far as a murder," he said. "Who did she kill? This Karl Lewis?"

"Oh, no," Chris said quickly. "Jan didn't kill anybody. It was Lewis who . . ." She glanced down and discovered the drink in her hand and tasted it. A drop of water, condensed on the cold glass, dropped on her skirt, and she rubbed at it with her fingers. "We were interested, naturally, because we'd been there the week before," she said in a low, even voice. "This man was killed behind the place, in the alley. Early in the morning. He was some kind of a crook or racketeer, in the black market, I think. Some columnist got hold of the fact that Karl Lewis had been questioned about the murder. He had produced an alibi." She hesitated and turned the glass in her hands. "The alibi was Jane Gordon, Hugh."

"Did they say she had been living with him?"

"It was . . . apparently it was one of those things that everybody in Hollywood knew about. I'm sorry. . . ."

He said bitterly, "I suppose your mother recognized her, too?" Everybody had known about his wife but him.

"I don't know. I don't think so. She never said, and I never asked because I didn't want to talk about it."

"Jan asked you to keep quiet about it?"

Chris nodded. "She said . . . she said that you would kill her if you learned about it."

"The number of people who would kill Janice," he said dryly, "or whom Janice would kill, if such and such happened. . . ."

Then he stopped, because Janice had been killed, and it was not really funny. Nothing was really funny any longer, and Chris was looking at him strangely. She put her glass aside and bent over to fasten up the buttons of her skirt, preparatory to leaving. He watched her fasten them and smooth the buttoned skirt over her hips and look up at him. There was a small stiff pause.

Chris asked quietly, "Are you sure you didn't know all this, Hugh?"

He had a sensation of danger. "I didn't know," he said carefully. "Why do you keep asking, Chris?"

The answer was at the back of his mind, but he would not let himself believe it. It went with the way she had acted and the way she had looked at him, as if she was afraid of him; and with the questions she had asked; but he did not want to believe it. Even after she had said it, he could not quite make himself believe it.

"Are you . . . sure you didn't kill her, Hugh?"

Then her voice, up to now quite steady, became breathless and frightened. "She said you would kill her if you found out! And *you* called it murder, Hugh! Nobody else! You!"

She moved backward away from him to the door, and stood in the doorway, waiting for him to reach her. When he moved his hands a little, perhaps merely to prevent her from fleeing, perhaps to shake sense into her, she shrank away from him. Then she stood quite still, but it was obvious that she was afraid of him. He stood with his hands at his sides, watching her fear.

"I didn't kill her," he said. It seemed ridiculous to have to say it.

"No," Chris whispered. "I . . . I know . . . something just made me. . . ."

She whirled blindly, fleeing from him and from what she was thinking about him, and scratched her bare sun-burned leg on the rough bark by the door, and stopped abruptly, bending over to rub the injury. Then, straightening up, she glanced at him still standing there. She walked across the porch, pushed the screen door aside, and walked out into the sunlight, but she was running again before she had gone out of sight around the corner of the house.

He knew that she was quite sure he had killed Janice. He knew suddenly that she had suspected it ever since he had told her that Janice had been murdered; and everything he had said today had confirmed her suspicions. *They'll remember that you didn't get along too well,* the black-haired man had warned him. *They'll remember that the last anybody saw you together you were both pretty mad at each other.* You had to hand it to Mr. Holt. Whatever else he was, he was a pretty smart man.

VIII

A spotlight was shining on the girl in the black satin gown as she sang. He could see her singing but he could not hear her. He tried to reach her, and the people in the audience held him back and shouted at him to sit down. He struggled forward through thickets of grasping hands, but the girl, still singing voicelessly, receded faster than he could follow, toward a door where a man was waiting for her, holding an object that cast a long cross-shaped shadow. He tried to call out to the girl, to warn her, but he could not think of the name of the thing the man was holding. Then the door closed.

He was kneeling beside her on the dead leaves, and her white dress was torn and dirty, and she was dead.

"Are you sure you didn't kill her, Hugh?" a girl's voice asked him.

He said no, he didn't kill her; and then suddenly he knew that he was not sure.

He woke up.

It was not quite dark in the room. Moonlight through the window shone on the gun and the pictures on the desk. He remembered waiting a long time after Chris was gone; then coming in here to lie down because his head ached. It still ached. He looked at the luminous electric clock on the desk; it read after nine. He got up and took the gun in his hands and sat down on the rumpled Navaho blanket covering the studio couch, holding the gun tightly while his heart gradually stopped pounding, but he did not stop being frightened.

He rubbed his fingers over the rough checkered walnut of the revolver butt. The war was still not so far away but that he could get a sense of reassurance from the feel of the weapon; you were never quite alone as long as you had a gun.

He remembered once, when she had driven to Baltimore, waiting late at night for her to come back. Suddenly he found himself listening expectantly for the telephone to ring to tell him that she had had an accident. He remembered the sick sense of horror with which he realized that he had been thinking calmly, almost hopefully, of what his life would be like if she were dead. . . . He remembered the evening she had thrown the ashtray at him; and as he braced himself to strike her he had seen the fireplace behind her, the andirons, the fender, and the hard smooth bricks of the hearth. He had seized her instead of striking her, not because he loved her and was afraid she might be hurt, but because, even through his anger, he had suddenly realized that should she fall and hurt herself he would never be quite sure that he had not deliberately struck hard enough to make it happen. For an instant he had known that he had wanted it to happen.

"But I didn't," he whispered. "And I never would have." But he had wanted it. Not to kill her, but simply to be rid of her.

He got up, turned on the light on the desk, and looked at the smiling studio photograph; and he knew that for days he had been hiding from himself the fact that he was glad she was gone. Chris had seen through the act the very first time they were together after the accident. She must have thought he was deliberately trying to conceal his relief; she must have wondered why he should feel the need for pretending to be broken-hearted; she had not realized that he was deceiving himself much better than he was deceiving her. Seeing him pretending to a grief much greater than he had any reason for feeling, she must have begun to wonder a little, remembering how things had actually been between him and Janice. And then, after she had commented on his behavior, he had volunteered a fairly implausible story of murder by an unknown truck-driver, as if to forestall any suspicions that might have risen in her mind. . . .

He stared at the smiling lovely face in the picture; and even then his sense of guilt tried to tell him that he could not stand to look at it; he had loved her so much; but he knew it was not true. He missed her, of course, as you would miss anybody you had got used to living with; but he had wanted to be rid of her and now, although he would have preferred to have it happen some other way, he was relieved that she was gone. It gave him a nasty sense of disloyalty to admit it at last, but he knew that it was the truth.

But it did not mean that he had killed her, he told himself. After all, he knew perfectly well what had happened. He had seen it all. He closed his eyes and saw it again, Janice in the glare of the headlight and the man in the shadow, then coming forward as she turned away to return to the car. . . . He could see every detail of it. He could almost see the man's face. He could see too much of it. He had thought about it so long that his mind had filled in the gaps and he no longer knew what was true and what he had made up to complete the picture. . . . It had been night when it happened but the picture showed everything, the hillside and the road as he had seen them later, when the snub-nosed girl in the yellow dress drove him out there. He could even see an election poster on a tree at the roadside, although it should not have been visible from below.

He could see it all, but he could not remember when he had wrenched himself free and cut the gash in his leg that had required nine stitches to close. He could not be sure that the face of the man was not his own face. He could not be sure that it was not he, Hugh Phillips, at whom Janice was screaming hysterically. . . . Perhaps the truck-driver had come down with his wrench and had seen them both lying there apparently dead, and had fled. Perhaps Janice, reviving, had got to the car and helped him out and, both half drunk and dazed with shock, they had quarreled . . . then his mind had rejected what had happened, telling him that he had never left the car until she was dead, seizing on the truck-driver as a scapegoat. . . .

If the wrench had killed her you would have thought the police surgeon would have noticed the wound. But Mr. Holt had said a rock. Phillips shivered suddenly, recalling all the black-haired man had said. It seemed to him, as he thought of the strange conversation again, that the man from the sheriff's office had been covertly threatening him, warning him that he, Mr. Holt, knew what had happened; that there was no evidence that would stand up in court but that Mr. Holt wanted Hugh Phillips to know that he had not got away with it and that sooner or later Mr. Holt expected him to confess. . . . *I don't like murder any more than you do,* Mr. Holt had said. *You'd rather she'd just died in an accident, wouldn't you?* Mr. Holt had known. Mr. Holt had warned him. *Murder is something you never get away from, once it has touched you.* . . . Everything the black-haired man had said fell into place and made sense when you looked at it like that. Mr. Holt had simply not realized that he had not known what had happened, that his mind had automatically protected him from the knowledge that he was a murderer. Mr. Holt had thought that he was consciously lying.

He found himself outside the house, walking slowly

through the moonlight; then his feet were on the stairs and he could see the boats and the dock below him. He had to get away from the house that he had shared with her. There was a fresh sailing breeze on the bay; he could hear it in the trees on the bluff, but the pier was sheltered inside the mouth of the river. The bay had a pale brilliance in the moonlight.

He found that he was still holding the gun. He put it down on the boards of the dock, but realized that somebody might see it there. Chris might come back and see the gun there and the boat gone and think, knowing what she did, that he had exchanged one method of suicide for another. He picked up the revolver and turned it, moved by a slow curiosity, until he could look into the round muzzle. The moonlight showed him the lands and grooves of the rifling, and the high target sight, and the gray lead noses of the bullets in the chambers of the cylinder. He grimaced and turned the weapon away from him. He was only, he knew, showing himself how lousy he felt as, under other conditions, he might have thrown a book across the room to show himself how mad he was. He did not, he discovered, feel nearly lousy enough to kill himself.

He tucked the weapon inside his belt, under his jacket, threw off the mooring lines, jumped aboard, and pushed off, letting the boat drift gently out toward the center of the river while he raised the sails. There was only a little water in the bilge and he tried to realize that it was only yesterday that Chris had come down the bluff while he was bailing. It seemed much longer. He sat on the deck by the tiller and lit a cigarette and nursed the boat toward the open water of the bay on the erratic breaths of wind that dipped over the bluff. The high banks made it a hell of a place to take a sailboat out of.

Then the sails filled solidly and he was easing himself out to weather and she was sailing. Looking back, he could see a light at the Hartshornes' up the river; it seemed to stare after him even when he was clear of the land and the mouth of the river had faded into the blackness of the shore. He wondered if Chris had gone there or if she had walked all the way home. He thought she would have walked home. She would not, he thought, have wanted to see anybody after what had happened. He put the boat about for the long tack down the bay and after a while the bulk of Sand Point cut off everything behind him.

The Brandons' was dark; the Carrs' also: they had not been out that summer and the people who had rented the place had left. There were scattered lights farther down the shore. There was a light at the Wellses'. He found himself tempted to let the boat bear off toward it. If he could talk to somebody. . . . But Chris could not reassure him. She believed he had done it.

He put about again, heading out into the bright moonlight toward the Eastern Shore, several miles away. The wind was strong enough now that he had to ease the little boat through the puffs, balancing her with the weight of his body, in the dark with the spray coming over, the boat pitching and plunging against the steep bay chop. The lights became smaller astern and he was alone in the moonlight. There was nothing else on the bay. He could drown out here and nobody would know it until his body came ashore. A sharp gust drove the edge of the deck under water. He eased the main sheet so that the mainsail spilled its wind, and the boat rose again, driving into the short sharp waves that sent luminous explosions of spray across the forward deck.

"Listen, bud," he said to himself aloud. "Listen, bud, a little Freud goes a long way."

The spray and the wind had cleared the sodden hopelessness from his mind. After all, he told himself, the fact that Chris suspected him did not prove anything except that he had acted like a damn fool. And what Mr. Holt thought was not proof, either; and he did not know what Mr. Holt thought. If Mr. Holt had known anything definite, Hugh Phillips would be in jail. And it was unpleasant to have to admit that he was relieved that Janice was dead; it made him feel like a particularly repulsive type of hypocrite, when he thought of the theatrical agonies he had put himself through to show himself how much he had loved her; but merely being fed up with a person did not mean that you had killed them. . . .

He shivered a little and looked around him in the moonlit darkness with the sudden realization that he did not have any idea where he was; then Cresset Point light blazed out to windward. Its bearing showed him he was too damn far out for a man just out of the hospital. He tacked and let the boat fall off until she was racing along with the wind just forward of the beam. No more spray struck him. He found that he was cold and rather wet and that nevertheless the thought of getting back to Sand Point gave him no pleasure. There might be a fire in the big fireplace at the Wellses'; there would be somebody to talk to; but Chris thought him a murderer.

A buoy came out of the darkness ahead. He could make out the white deposits the seagulls had left on it, and the number: 35A. It was the buoy off Polling Creek. He remembered, suddenly, a slight snub-nosed girl running lightly across the grass in the sunshine.

Changing course, he told himself that he was a fool and that she would probably be startled and certainly very puzzled at having a strange, half-soaked young man drop in on her by water in the middle of the night. Her father would be even more puzzled. They would probably think he was delirious and insist on driving him home and getting him a doctor. He grinned at the thought. Suddenly he was almost happy.

At the mouth of Polling Creek a reedy spit made a shadow on the water, reaching out from the shore to the right as he came in; and from this spit, he knew, a long submerged sandbar extended a hundred yards toward the steep dark bank of the opposite shore, half closing the entrance. But in the small centerboard boat he did not have to worry about the depth of the water. He coasted in with the wind aft, gradually losing it as the shores enveloped him. The centerboard struck bottom, popped up in its trunk, bounced a few times while the reeds slid past to starboard, and dropped down again. Safe in deep water, he jibed the sails over and stood up toward the first dock in the cove ahead, where the trees on the high bank seemed to overhang the shore. There was a light in the cottage behind the trees.

He luffed, and a small gust of wind reached into the creek to rattle the sails loudly; then he had them down on deck. The momentum carried the boat alongside the dock. He thought it was a pretty neat landing.

He tied up astern of a small outboard runabout, the large motor of which was tilted clear of the water and secured to the boat and the dock with a heavy padlocked chain.

As he climbed stiffly to the dock he heard a screen door slam in the cottage above. He stood waiting, feeling gingerly of the seat of his slacks, wet with the spray that had run along the deck. The girl came to the head of the stairs above him and stood looking down at him. She was still wearing the embroidered black peasant skirt and the thin white blouse that she had worn earlier in the day at Sand Point, and the wind blew the full skirt against her legs as she stood there.

It gave him a curious feeling to see her waiting for him up there, alone, as if she had known he was coming. It seemed as if both of them had known he would come. He limped along the dock toward the stairs. The cramped quarters of the cockpit had made his leg quite painful, and he could feel a dozen bruises he had thought to be healed. She waited for him at the head of the stairs in the moonlight. She did not move at all, except once to brush at a strand of her hair blown across her face by the wind, until he reached her. Then she stepped back to let him up.

"Isn't it rather late to be out sailing, Mr. Phillips?" she asked, smiling.

He was catching his breath from the climb and did not answer. It made him feel awkward to be so weak. He had felt no lack of strength while he was sailing, but now he felt drained and empty, and he wanted to sit down.

The girl's face became worried. "Should you go out alone like that, so soon after . . . ? I mean, if anything happened, you wouldn't be able to swim very far. . . ."

"I've never drowned yet," he said.

"I heard your sails," she said. "Dad's gone to Washington. I . . ." She laughed. ". . . Sometimes I get to listening when I'm here alone."

"I know," he said.

Something in his voice made her glance at him quickly. "Is anything the matter?"

He looked down at her face in the moonlight and thought that it was strange the number of different ways that girls had of being attractive. He liked the incongruity between the snub-nosed face and the slender, leggy figure; snub-nosed girls were generally quite small and often plump.

He could not seem to catch his breath completely, and he reached out to support himself by one of the two-by-fours of the stairway railing. A growing roaring in his ears became stronger than the sound of the wind in the trees around them; and suddenly he was desperately frightened at the way his head hurt, as if there were something wrong with it.

He looked at the girl again and her face did not look the same; it had a blunt, blurred, animal-like quality, and there was something sinuous and boneless in the way she moved, coming toward him. He told himself that it was part of going crazy to imagine everyone against you, but he drew back instinctively. In his mind, as his foot slipped, he saw the precipitous stairs behind him; then he was falling.

The girl caught his arm. He felt himself half turned in the air and he sat down heavily on the top step.

• "Don't . . ." Shirley Carlson was saying breathlessly. "Don't try to get up. Just sit there for a moment. . . ."

He could feel her hand still gripping his arm. He could not bring himself to look at her face as she knelt beside him. In the moonlight he could see her shoulders and the very fresh clean straps of her undergarments through the almost transparent material of her blouse; but they looked innocent and unprovocative.

She rose abruptly and put her hands under his armpits and tried to lift him back from the stairs. She was not nearly strong enough, and suddenly he found himself laughing.

"Cut it out," he gasped. "Cut it out. I'm ticklish. . . ."

He turned his head to look up at her as she let him go. Her face was quite all right again, but it looked almost angry.

"You were afraid of me!" she said accusingly. "You thought I was going to push you!"

He felt himself flush, and he tried to rise. She took his arm quickly.

"Are you sure you're all right?" When he nodded, she went on breathlessly, "You did. I could see it in your face. You thought . . ."

He did not deny it. "I'm sorry. Things have been a little mixed up lately."

"I'm going to take you up to the house," Shirley Carlson said. "And when you feel all right I'm going to drive you home. . . ."

"I thought you said your father had gone to Washington. . . ."

Suddenly he was flushing again, and she had turned to look at him. He could see the quick hurt and anger in her face.

She said quietly, "Yes, but he didn't take the car, Mr. Phillips. Some people down the road drove him in their car." He could see her mouth tremble as she tried to smile. "Would you care to search the premises?" He did not say anything. She went on, "I wish I knew what that sheriff man had told you about me."

He frowned. "He didn't say anything about you."

"Well, somebody must have said something. Every time we meet you accuse me of something, Mr. Phillips. It's true I did lie about what I saw that night and you were very smart to catch me at it, but really, my father isn't hiding in the bushes so if you came here to kill me with that gun . . ."

His hand went to his waist. He had forgotten all about the weapon but it was still there. The girl faced him stiffly.

"Yes, it's rather obvious, isn't it? And I'm quite alone.

So if you want to kill me because it was my fault that your wife . . ."

"Shut up!" he whispered. He could feel himself trembling as if he had been cold as long as he could remember. He could see the girl watching him steadily, and the look in her eyes was horribly familiar, because he had seen the same look in the eyes of Christine Wells. She was afraid of him.

"Oh, it was my fault," the girl whispered. "I didn't mean it, but it was my fault. . . ."

"Damn it, shut up!" He licked his lips. "Do I *look* like a murderer? You're the second person tonight. . . ." He saw her eyes widen, and he laughed. "Oh, no. I haven't killed anybody. She accused me of murdering Janice. My wife." Then he said very quickly, "After she'd gone, I had a nightmare and I woke up scared stiff and the gun . . . Then I had to get out of the house and I just sort of brought it along. I'd have left it in the boat if I'd remembered about it."

He saw the fear gradually go out of her eyes as she studied his face. She laughed a little uncertainly.

"I'm afraid I didn't follow all that, Mr. Phillips. But I obviously can't let you out in that boat again tonight. You'd better come up to the house and have something to eat, and then I'll drive you home. You can come back for your boat some other time."

He said, "Well, if you're going to adopt me, you might as well call me Hugh."

IX

Inside the cottage the furniture was varnished maple, scratched and chipped by generations of summer residents. The rugs were threadbare and the walls had not been papered since before the war. Someone at some time, not recently, had painted over the paper with pale green paint of the kind you mix with water. There was a half-packed suitcase on the living-room davenport and another visible, on the bed, through the open bedroom door.

"You're leaving?" Phillips asked, turning to look at the girl, who had stopped by the mirror in the small hallway to smooth her hair.

She said, "Yes, Dad's almost through in Washington. We're starting back for St. Louis in the morning."

It disturbed him to think of her leaving. He stood waiting in the middle of the living room, feeling faintly embarrassed, as if they were lovers who had come down to this place to spend, for the first time, a weekend together. It was getting to be quite late at night and she was a very attractive girl. He watched her pat the hair at her temples and settle it into place with a small shake of her head.

"What business is your father in?" he asked.

"Filters," she said. "Oil filters, you know, for cars. He had a contract with the government during the war and now he's all wound up in red tape. . . . You know how things are in Washington." She turned from the mirror to smile at Phillips. "I don't know anything about it, really. I just came down to keep house for him. He wanted to try to sneak in a little vacation while he was seeing people, that's why we took this place instead of staying in Washington." She looked at the dingy room and smiled again. "Isn't it awful?"

"Are you glad or sorry to be leaving?" he asked.

"Oh, it's been nice," she said, coming forward. She laughed at the tone of her voice. "I mean, it gets a little lonely in a place like this when you don't know anybody. . . ." Then, as if she had said more than she had intended, she walked quickly to the davenport, and closed the suitcase, waving him back. "Please sit down. It isn't heavy."

"You know," he said, "tonight makes the second time you've saved my life."

He heard her laugh in the bedroom. "I do make a habit of it, don't I?" She came out, closing the door behind her. "You look chilly. Why don't you light the fire while I get something in the kitchen. . . . Do you take coffee?"

"Sure," he said.

"I didn't know. Some people won't take it at night. They think it keeps them awake. . . ." She stood with her back to the door, frowning a little. At last she smiled. "I was just trying to think whether you'd said anything about being hungry."

He heard himself burst into a loud spontaneous laugh and he knew that he felt better than he had for a long time. She was laughing with him.

"Perhaps I just assumed it," she said at last. "But you are, aren't you? My mother used to say that . . ." She hesitated and glanced at him quickly, almost shyly, ". . . that if you didn't know what to do with a man you could always feed him. . . . I'll be right back."

He watched her flee from the room, and laughed, and turned to the fireplace. When the paper was alight he backed away and watched the fire spread to the kindling with a growing roar. He stripped off his damp coat and felt the heat through his shirtsleeves. He hung the coat over the back of a chair to dry and took the gun from his belt and laid it on the mantelpiece. Shirley Carlson came into the room with a large tray which she set on the end table by the davenport. She sat down beside it.

"Dad ought to be getting back pretty soon," she said. "I always fix him a snack when he gets home. I hope you like tuna-fish salad. Please sit down. Maybe you'd like something to drink. I didn't think to ask. . . ."

He said, a little stiffly, "It's getting pretty late. I guess I should be getting home."

She looked up, startled. After a moment she smiled. "I'm sorry. Was I acting . . . ?"

"Just a little," he said. "As if you were telling yourself firmly that the crazy man wasn't going to hurt you as long as you humored him."

"I didn't mean to." She laughed. "Please sit down, Hugh. It's just that, well, out in St. Louis we've kind of got in the habit of leaving our shootin' arns home when we go visiting." She brushed back her hair and leaned back against the davenport cushions, looking up at him. She said frankly, "I mean, I'm not very brave, and this place gives me the creeps, anyway, if you want to know; and when a strange sailboat comes gliding up to the dock in the middle of the night and the fellow in it is carrying a gun and thinks I want to shove him down a flight of stairs and talks about being accused of murder . . . Well, it's not very reassuring to an innocent maiden from the Middle West, Hugh."

He drew a large chair within reach and sat down. She gave him a plate and poured a cup of coffee for him.

"Do you want to tell me?" she murmured. "Or shouldn't I ask?"

"Would you feel better if I left?" he asked.

"Well," she said, laughing a little. "I would feel *safer*." He frowned and she touched his knee fleetingly. "Don't worry about it. Do you take cream or sugar?"

"Both," he said. ". . . That's plenty."

He took the cup and looked up to see her eyes studying his face gravely.

"Who thinks you're a murderer, Hugh?" she asked. "Why should anybody think you'd killed your wife? After all, it was obviously an accident. . . ."

He opened his mouth to tell her about the truck-driver and the wrench and the words would not come. He had told the story twice and neither time had the reception been notably successful. He found that he did not want to tell this girl a story that he was not sure of, himself, any longer.

"You've been reading too many detective stories," he said. "In real life nobody pays much attention to what actually happened, because only those who saw it can be sure it actually happened. I mean, she read in the papers that Janice had been killed. She didn't see it happen. All she knows is that I said it happened. You said it happened, but she doesn't know you. You're just a name to her. The police say it happened but you know the cops, they're always being fooled. All she really knows is that Jan is dead."

"This is a girl you know?"

Phillips glanced up quickly. "Oh. Sorry. Yes, her name's Christine Wells. I've known her all my life."

"You're in love with her?" Shirley Carlson asked, smiling.

He laughed. "Obvious question. No, I was once. I was going to marry her. Then I married Jan instead. . . . The night she was killed, Jan accused Chris and me of, well, you can fill it in. Jan was a little tight and it was a nasty scene. There wasn't any truth in what she was saying. I was pretty sore at her for making a fool of herself like that. Chris must have seen that. The next morning she hears that Jan got killed on the way home."

Shirley frowned thoughtfully. "There must be more to it than that. Nobody would come out and accuse somebody they had known for a long time . . ."

"Well, everybody knew we hadn't been getting along. And I acted like a damn fool. I didn't want to admit to myself that I . . ." He grimaced and dug at the plate on his knee, ". . . that I was glad she was dead," he said, without looking up.

"Oh!"

"That's a hell of a thing to have to say, isn't it? You're the first person I've said it to."

The girl looked up slowly. Her eyes were very wide and shocked. "It must have been dreadful for you when you realized it."

"I didn't realize it until Chris accused me. . . . But I did act like a damn fool, Shirley. I didn't have to go around pretending to be broken-hearted. . . . I hope you don't mind my unloading all this on you. It must seem kind of funny. . . ."

"No," she said. "No. It doesn't. At all." She shook her head minutely. Then she smiled at him. "But it should, shouldn't it?"

"I hope your dad won't think I . . ." He glanced at the clock over the mantelpiece and saw the gun and grimaced. He set his plate aside, rose, took the gun down and put it on the chair that held his coat, hiding it under a fold of the coat. "Anyway," he said, returning, "I was acting kind of funny and it was I who suggested that it might be murder."

"Hugh!"

He looked at her bleakly. "I can't tell you exactly . . . I had reasons . . . I'm not quite sure . . ." He gulped his coffee. "But you can see that Chris might put things together that way, once I had mentioned murder. . . ."

"But why?" She was watching him breathlessly, almost frightened again. "Why should *you* think . . . ?"

Suddenly he saw things very clearly. He saw that the truck-driver, even without a wrench in his hand, was still a very questionable figure. He saw that even if he, Hugh Phillips, had never seen anything between the time the car went over and the time he woke up in the hospital, he would still, now, have had to face the fact that Janice might have been murdered. Because it was straining coincidence to the bounds of reason to believe that a girl who had been involved in one murder, and who had later acquired a large sum of money in some way that she had not wanted anybody to know about, should shortly thereafter die accidentally under circumstances that were not ordinary.

After all, under ordinary circumstances, the truck-driver would not have fled. Truck-drivers were respectable men who knew the laws better than ordinary drivers; they were used to seeing highway accidents; they were not especially noted for being easily shocked into panic. Better than most drivers, they knew the penalties for leaving the scene of an accident. Furthermore, better than most drivers, they knew where you should and should not park. Regardless of what Hugh Phillips had or had not seen later, he had certainly seen a large van standing in the center of the east-bound lane of the Washington-Annapolis highway just around a blind curve where no man with good sense would have left it.

If there had been nothing but a vanishing truck, and a murder that could have been the hallucination of a half-unconscious young man who wanted to be rid of his wife, then you could have accepted it. But when you tied it to another murder, and to the suspicion of blackmail, it became just a little too much to swallow.

He pushed back the flickering gleam of hope that had come into his mind, and examined the theory gingerly, half afraid to look at it closely for fear it would come apart and show him that he was only, once more, trying to escape from the knowledge of his own guilt. After all, he was simply doing what Chris had done. He was constructing a murder that might have happened because somebody might have wanted it to happen, without regard to the facts.

He could hear the wind blowing outside, rustling the leaves of a tree at the window at the end of the room with a steady sound, almost like rain. The fireplace made small popping, sputtering sounds. The clock on the brick mantelpiece read a quarter of twelve, but time did not mean anything any longer. Time had stopped quite a while ago, when Chris accused him of murder.

He saw Shirley watching him uncertainly, puzzled and a little afraid.

He said, "I want you to think about what happened that night."

She opened her mouth to ask a question, caught herself, and clasped her skirt over her knees, studying her hands.

"I don't know what I can tell you, Hugh." Her voice said that she did not understand, but that she was willing to try to help him. "I was driving about forty, I guess, and then I saw this truck. . . ."

"No," he said. "Back further. Did you see anything before that?"

She looked up abruptly. "No, should I have?" She frowned. "Well, just before, I met a big car, it must have been doing eighty, but that was before. . . ."

He felt his hands close tightly, and tried not to let elation show on his face. He remembered Janice's anger when the big car passed them.

"Yes," he said, "yes, that's one thing."

"I don't understand."

"I'll tell you in a minute," he said. "I don't want to put

ideas into your head. Think about the truck. Was it moving?"

She shook her head. "No." Then she said carefully, "That is, of course I thought it was when I saw the lights, and I slowed down because the bridge at the bottom is rather narrow and I didn't want to meet anybody on it. I wanted to let them get over it first; but then I saw it was just standing there on the hill. . . ."

"Are you quite sure it wasn't moving?"

She closed her eyes and he could see her trying to visualize the way the lights had been on the road that night. With her eyes closed she looked extremely young; it was as if her eyes were a little older than the rest of her face. She opened them again and looked at him.

"I'm sorry, Hugh. I really can't remember. It might have been when I first saw it."

He leaned forward in the big chair and asked, *"Could it have been going backward?"*

She stared at him. Her small square face looked quite shocked at the idea. "Oh, no! No, I would have noticed *that!"* After a long silence she said, "I'm sorry. Did I say something wrong?"

He did not answer at once. Then he said, "No, it's all right. It doesn't have to be backward." He leaned forward again, speaking eagerly. "Look, Shirley, I think Jan was murdered. Can you just accept that for a moment? Don't think about it, just accept it. Now think of the way that truck was standing there, just below the curve, so that anybody coming down the hill fast would burst around the curve and not have time to do anything about it. Well, they couldn't leave the truck there indefinitely. Anybody might have piled into it. It must have been waiting either above the curve or well below it. If it had been waiting below, then it would have had to back into position. You might have seen it from the other side, as you came down toward the bridge. . . ."

She shook her head minutely. "No." Her mouth was strained. "And the big car, Hugh?"

"Somebody had to pass the word that we were coming, so that the truck could move into place."

She had put her cup and plate aside. Now she stood up quickly, with a movement that was almost a shudder. She stood looking down into his face.

"No," she whispered. "No. You mustn't start thinking things like that, Hugh. It's . . . that's the way people go crazy." She brushed sharply at the folds of her skirt and looked at him again. "I know it was awful," she said softly, "but you mustn't let yourself . . . *Don't you see what you're saying?*" she cried. "You have a truck and a driver and a big car and somebody driving that . . . all just to kill your wife, Hugh, it's . . ."

"Crazy," he said, rising.

She caught his arms, holding him tightly, almost shaking him. "Yes," she said, "it's crazy."

They stood for a long moment like that; then she let her hands fall.

"Hugh," she said, "haven't you forgotten something?"

He frowned.

"Me?" she whispered. "You've forgotten me, haven't you, Hugh? Or have you? Is that why you came here? I was the cork in the bottle, wasn't I? It was my stupidity that didn't give you a chance. If it hadn't been for me coming up the hill and stopping my car just there . . ."

He said sharply, "No. Now *you're* being . . ."

"That's really why you came here, isn't it?" she gasped. "That's why . . ." She swallowed. "That's why you thought I was going to push you, out there. *You think I'm . . .*"

"Stop it!" he said, taking her by the shoulders.

"I won't!" She tried to push his hands away. "Don't you see, Hugh? Either I'm in it or it doesn't make sense! Whoever you think is doing these insane things, they couldn't afford to leave a hole like that; they couldn't count on your going so fast that you couldn't turn. And certainly they couldn't count on bright little Shirley parking her car just where it would do the most good; I've got to be in it, Hugh, if what you're saying is . . ." She caught her breath sharply. The sound was very close to a sob. "Hugh, I was *there*," she whispered. "Can't you see how it sounds when you tell *me* it was murder?"

He licked his lips, looking down at her. "Aren't you taking an awful chance, Shirley?"

She watched him steadily.

He said, "Suppose I believed you. Suppose you convinced me that you . . . Here you are alone in the house and it's past midnight. . . ."

She smiled very suddenly. "It is pretty late, isn't it? You'd better kill me quick or my reputation will be hopelessly compromised."

Then her smile changed quality and he knew that he was going to kiss her, and that she knew it, and he did.

X

He could not put away the feeling that at any moment Janice would walk in and find them there. He knew exactly the way her mouth would twitch into a small contemptuous smile, and he knew what she would say: something hard and bright and not particularly original. She would probably begin by apologizing for interrupting them. . . .

"What's the matter?"

Shirley's face looked very young and almost beautiful in the soft light from the lamp on the table at the far end of the davenport. He was very much aware of her presence very close to him; the fragile stuff of her blouse was faintly harsh under his hand on her shoulder. He kissed the top of her head absently.

"I'm sorry. I guess it hasn't been long enough to . . . I can't help feeling that she's going to walk in."

He felt her shiver a little. She sat up beside him and touched her hair, but did not move out of the circle of his arm. He found a pack of cigarettes in his shirt pocket and offered it to her.

"No, I don't smoke," she said.

There was always a tone of moral superiority in the

voices of people who told you that they did not smoke. He was sure that she had not meant it; and then he was not so certain. It was possible that she felt ashamed of herself for allowing a man who was almost a stranger to kiss her, and for allowing herself to respond to his kiss. It was possible that she was trying to make it perfectly clear that she was a nice girl.

He put a cigarette between his lips and lit it clumsily, one-handed, and listened to the wind. When you wanted to go sailing on a bright afternoon there was always a flat calm; but when you were afraid at night there was always a wind blowing, so that you could not hear anything but the wind and the leaves of the trees rustling in the dark around you. He did not know what he was afraid of. He knew that he felt guilty and disloyal, and that he and the girl beside him had shared something for a moment, but it had gone away.

"Hadn't you better tell me, darling?" Shirley said. "Maybe if you talked about it. . . ."

He glanced at her. It reassured him to look at her face. "All right," he said. "There was a picture. . . ." He told her about the picture and the bank book and Chris's story. Shirley listened thoughtfully, without moving.

"And you think," she said at last, "that your wife gave this man an alibi and then got afraid of him and ran away. . . ."

He nodded.

She went on, "And after she'd married you she began to feel secure enough to ask the man for money. . . . Hugh, have you any proof that there *was* another murder aside from . . ."

"Aside from what Chris said? No, but why should she. . . ?" He stopped and looked at her quickly.

Shirley moved a little. "I don't know anything about it, darling, but . . . is Christine rich?"

Phillips said stiffly, "They've got plenty of money. Her father's a captain in the Navy and I think he's got a private income; I know Mrs. Wells has some money of her own. But . . ."

"Please let me talk, Hugh." She caught his hand. "Let

me just say it. I know you don't want to hear it, but I've been listening to what you told me, and it's all Christine, darling. She's the one who got . . . jilted. She's the one your wife made a scene about. She's the one who saw your wife on the West Coast. . . . Doesn't that seem like a coincidence to you? Suppose your wife, Janice, had learned something about Christine out there instead of the other way around. Suppose Janice came east and deliberately married you so that she could be near . . ."

"No," he said, but it was just the sort of thing that Janice would delight in doing. To steal the fiancé of the girl she was blackmailing. . . . Shirley's voice went on.

"Doesn't it seem strange to you that Christine should 'recognize' Janice almost a year after—"

"No," he said.

He felt his hand released. "You're in love with her, aren't you?"

"I've known her all my life. Mrs. Wells and the Captain are both swell people."

"You are," Shirley whispered. "You want to prove that your wife was murdered, but the minute I suggest . . ." She sat up straight, away from contact with his arm. "I think . . . I think you really came here with some crazy notion that I—"

He paid no attention to her. "Listen," he said. "Listen, she wouldn't have accused me if . . ."

Shirley was silent; and he found his own answer. If Chris could make him believe that she thought him guilty, she could be sure there was no question in his mind of her own innocence.

He shook his head abruptly. "No. No, I don't buy that, Shirley."

He could feel her eyes regarding him. "No, I didn't think you would. . . . But I had to say it." He heard her breath catch momentarily. "After all, it doesn't have to be murder, darling. . . ."

He pushed Chris out of his mind with an effort. He wondered if the boat were chafing against the pier below the cottage, but it was not a matter of great importance.

He wondered if there was still moonlight on the bay. He thought the wind was dying a little.

"You don't *know,*" Shirley said insistently. "Darling, you don't *know* it was murder."

"You don't understand," he said slowly, almost absently. "I saw it."

"Of course," she said, startled. "Of course, darling. So did I."

"No," he said, "you don't understand, Shirley." He could not call her darling. There had been a moment, but it was gone, and it seemed to him that Janice was listening. "You don't understand. I was lying there afterward, pinned in the car, and I saw it. You must have been on the way to the police station by then."

He saw the color leave her face. There were small freckles on the bridge of her upturned nose. He wondered why she should be frightened. He wished he had met her some other time, when whatever had gone wrong with them need not have happened.

"You mean . . ." Shirley licked her pale lips. "You mean . . . *she wasn't dead?*"

He frowned, not quite understanding the intensity with which she was watching him; then everything that had passed between them unreeled through his mind in a crazy patchwork of words and phrases and shades of expression. He remembered that he had caught her in a lie the very first time they talked together alone. She had claimed that, although she had not seen who was driving the car, nevertheless she had told Mr. Holt that it had been Janice, because she had been so sorry for him, Hugh Phillips, and had not wanted him to have any more trouble. No nice girl just driving past would have risked it for an unconscious man she did not know. She could not have been sure that, waking up, he would not confess and make a liar of her. No, but Shirley Carlson had known who was driving, even though she had not seen it, because her accomplice, the truck-driver, had told her.

And then, not quite sure how much he knew, she had picked him up after the inquest to find out.

He could not believe what he was thinking and he did

not dare to look at her. He heard himself speaking quietly.

"No, she wasn't dead, darling," he said, and the word came very easily now. "She was frightened, hysterical; she was hurt; she ran to the man for help and he struck her down with the wrench as you would swat a fly. And even then he wasn't sure so he knelt beside her and deliberately hit her again. I'll remember the sound of it all my—"

"No!"

The word had no more volume than a whisper, but it had the quality of a scream.

Everything in the room was very sharp and clear, with the fine wiry clarity of a good photograph, but when he looked at it, the girl's face looked blurred. It had the blunt, inhuman look that he had seen on it once before. He closed his fingers on her shoulder with abrupt brutality, holding her beside him.

"No!" she gasped. "No! You're lying! It wasn't like that. *He didn't . . . !*"

He wanted to take her throat in his hands and shake her until the smooth brown hair was a tangled mop and the small head flopped loose on the slender neck. He wanted to kill her. She saw it in his face.

"I mean," she panted, "I mean . . . it's so horrible . . . I can't believe . . . *Let me go!*"

She rose and plunged away from him and he felt the thin blouse come tearing away and, instinctively, released her at the embarrassing sensation of the frail material ripping under his fingers. She snatched the gun from the chair, and the chair fell over on the hearth with a loud crash as she turned.

The gun was large and lethal in her small hand. The blouse had fallen off her shoulders. It was strange, he thought, that a garment that had hidden so little should look so indecent when it was torn away. She ran her fingers abruptly through her hair, pushing it back from her face, irretrievably shattering the smooth cap of it into undisciplined strands. Her fingers moved stiffly down the side of her head, over her ear, and down the line of her jaw. She pressed them tightly against her mouth for a moment and pulled them away.

"Don't move," she gasped. "Don't move, you———!"

He did not catch the name she called him, but he did not think he had ever heard it before.

"You kissed me," she whispered. "What kind of a louse are you? I thought you knew. I couldn't figure your bringing a gun unless you knew. And then, by God, you kissed me!"

He licked his lips. "Why didn't you push me on the stairs?" he asked, watching the gun.

"I thought it was a gag. I thought you wanted to see if I'd . . ."

"I didn't know, Shirley," he said. "I didn't know until just now."

"I'm supposed to believe that?"

Suddenly she was crying. She pressed her hand against her mouth but she could not stop the choking sobs; her whole body was trembling, and she went to her knees on the threadbare rug and buried her face in her hands. He looked at her and wished that she did not look so very much like a small disheveled child crying because a larger child had beat her up.

He found himself ridiculously wanting to go to her and comfort her. He could not help a feeling of admiration as he realized the game she had played with him, he not once suspecting that it was a game: accusing herself recklessly, telling him the truth and making him laugh at it, accusing Christine. But she had been just a little too good. She had made herself such a nice girl that he had kissed her; and she had not been able to stand the inhuman strain of being made love to by a man she was not at all sure had not come there to kill her. He had felt her withdrawal but had not understood it.

He told himself that she had helped to kill Janice, even though apparently she had not been told everything that had happened. She had driven her car there, and had lied to the police. . . . But he could not bring back the momentary hate he had felt for her. He could only feel tremendously sorry for her and, a little, for himself; and grateful to her for finally dispelling the doubts he had had of himself.

The gun slid down her skirt to the floor. He rose to pick it up. Then the bedroom door closed gently but quite definitely and a tall man with gray hair was standing there, wearing a gray suit, white shoes, and holding a Colt .380 automatic.

"I wouldn't," Mr. Carlson said.

Phillips straightened up slowly and stood facing the tall man, holding his hands carefully away from his sides. It seemed to be a position you fell into naturally when a gun was pointed at you. He watched Mr. Carlson come forward, and remembered shaking hands with him earlier in the day. *I want you to meet my father,* Shirley Carlson had said. The whole scene, that he had thought nothing of at the time, took on a grim significance. The man, of course, was no more her father than he had been Janice's.

"You're . . ."

"That's right, kid. Lewis," the tall man said. "Karl Lewis. I used to know your wife."

"You killed her."

Karl Lewis nodded. "You saw me, didn't you, kid? Tough."

Without letting the gun waver, he reached down and dragged the girl up by one arm. "Pull yourself together, Kitten," he said, shaking her a little. "Get yourself a drink and a safety pin."

He released her and put two fingers between his lips and whistled shrilly. The footsteps of two men crossed the porch. The tall man spoke to the men before they entered the cottage.

"Everything is fine. Bring the Buick around and wait in it."

The footsteps went away. The girl drew a ragged breath and rubbed at her eyes with the back of her hand. The man glanced at her, but she pulled at her torn blouse and did not look at him.

"Karl, did you really . . . ?"

"Sure. It had to be done, didn't it?"

"Then why did you lie to me about it?"

"Lie?" He smiled. "I didn't lie, Kitten. I told you she was dead. You didn't ask for——"

"I said, it was lucky the one you wanted was killed and the one you didn't, wasn't. And you said yes, it was very lucky."

The man said nothing and the girl, after a moment, turned slowly away from him and walked to the cabinet by the fireplace. Still holding her blouse about her shoulders with her left hand, she took a bottle and a shot-glass from the cabinet, extracted the cork, filled the glass, drained it abruptly with a single motion, put it down, and wiped her fingers on her skirt.

She turned. "I just meant," she said carefully, "that if you'd told me I wouldn't have been so shocked when he said it. If you want me to act these parts for you, Karl, you've got to let me know what's going on. That's all I meant."

"I know, Kitten," the tall man said gently. "I know you wouldn't mean anything else."

The girl looked at him and her eyes held a sick uneasiness. Phillips could see her facing the brutal fact of murder for the first time and, perhaps, wondering when it would happen to her. A car forced off the road was just another accident, even if it had been made to happen. It was a nice remote kind of homicide for which no one person was directly responsible. You could not clearly visualize it happening to you. But a girl beat to death with a socket wrench. . . .

She poured the shot-glass full again and carried it across the room into the bedroom, and the door closed behind her. Karl Lewis studied the closed door for a moment. Then he bent down and picked up the long-barreled revolver lying at his feet.

"Well, so you did recognize me," he said to Hugh Phillips.

A big car pulled into the driveway outside. Its motor stopped and one man in it asked another for a light.

XI

Suddenly he was no longer a spectator. He had been
standing by the davenport, careful not to move, of course,
because of the gun, but feeling remote and only vaguely
concerned, as if watching a play on a distant stage. Then
the tall man checked the loads in the long-barreled revolver, dropped his own pistol into his pocket, and turned
his full attention on Hugh Phillips; and suddenly he was
in it, he was a part of it, and he was in danger.

"No," he said slowly. "No, I didn't recognize you."

"You said you would at the inquest. You were going to
identify me." Karl Lewis smiled.

Phillips remembered the idea he had had when Mr.
Holt asked him if he could identify the truck-driver; and
he felt a dim sense of triumph to know that it had, after
all, worked. Karl Lewis had been worried enough by the
statement that he had come over that afternoon to make
sure, one way or another, whether Phillips was a danger
to him. It occurred to Phillips that if he had acted only a
little differently, if he had shown any interest in Shirley
Carlson's 'father,' if he had thought up some excuse to go
with them as he had later regretted not having done, he
would very probably be dead now. Under the circumstances the escape seemed hardly worth getting worked
up about.

"I was bluffing," he said. "I thought there was a
chance that if the guy who had killed her thought I'd
know him . . ." He stopped, seeing Karl Lewis's expression change minutely, frowning; then the tall man was
smiling again.

"Smart. Or not so smart. If I hadn't thought you might
be trying to kid somebody you wouldn't be standing here
now. . . ."

The bedroom door opened and the girl stood in the

165

doorway, fastening the buttons of the crisp cotton shirt-waist with which she had replaced her ruined blouse. She did not say anything.

"You sent her to check up on me?" Phillips asked, moving his head minutely in her direction.

"Yeah, and to give me an excuse to drop around. She said you went back there looking for something, so I figured you had seen something. But if you couldn't recognize me, there still wasn't any point in . . ." He smiled gently. "But you didn't? This afternoon?"

Phillips shook his head. It seemed to him that the man was leading him somewhere, that Karl Lewis had been surprised when he denied having recognized him and was now probing for some important information; but he could not see what harm the truth would do. It did not seem to him, as he stared at the steady muzzle of his own gun, that things could very well be much worse than they were.

"You know I didn't," he said, wondering how it would come and where they were going to do it. Because there was no doubt that he could recognize the man now.

"But you saw something that night?"

"Yes."

"What did you see?"

"I saw you kill her," Phillips said. "But I never saw your face."

"Why didn't you tell the cops?"

"I did, but they thought I was crazy."

The tall man asked very softly, *"If you didn't recognize me, kid, how did you know enough to come here?"*

In the doorway, the girl had stopped moving as she waited for the answer.

Phillips looked back to the tall man. "I didn't know," he said, puzzled. "I just had to get out of the house. I came by here in the boat and remembered that she had been nice to me. . . . I had to talk to somebody. . . ."

Karl Lewis slapped him across the face so that he reeled back against the davenport and had to put a hand against the wall to steady himself. The blow started his head to aching again. He pushed himself blindly away from the wall and the tall man slapped him again, back-handed, and he sat down, feeling the belated pain explode behind his eyeballs and run through his head into the back of his neck. When he looked up, the tall man was watching him, his eyes very blue against the gray of his suit and hair. They were the color of a cheap blue china plate and had exactly as much expression.

"So you came with a gun," Karl Lewis said softly. "Try again, kid."

"I forgot . . ." he said. "I just happened to. . . ." It sounded improbable and a little undignified. It sounded as if he were making it up because he was frightened. "Go to hell," he said.

He parried a blow, and Karl Lewis rammed the muzzle of the revolver viciously into his stomach; and he gagged and doubled over. He heard the distant sound of the other's voice.

"You found something, didn't you?"

"Yes," he gasped. "A picture and a bank book. . . ."

"Yeah, I heard that story when you told Kitten here. And you still just dropped around to be sociable?"

It had slipped away from him again, and he was standing outside watching it, and it made him uncomfortable. The young man who was being beaten up should have been braver about it, because he was after all the hero of the piece. He tried to stand up and the tall man knocked him back to the davenport. He could taste blood in his mouth.

He caught his breath and said, "I really didn't suspect anything until she . . ."

His voice sounded like the voice of a nice little boy who had got into the wrong company and did not quite understand the joke that everyone was laughing at. Then he remembered that the house at Sand Point had been searched.

It was clear, at last, where the tall man was leading him; and why it would have been better to say that he had recognized the man that afternoon. It was clear that Karl Lewis, after killing Janice, had begun to wonder uneasily whether she might not have left some evidence.

He had searched the house and found nothing. Having later assured himself that, in spite of the evidence at the inquest, there was no one who could identify him, he had been packing, ready to leave, feeling himself secure and unsuspected; and suddenly the dead girl's husband, who had shown no signs of recognition earlier in the day, had turned up, carrying a gun.

The tall man's first thought had been that Phillips, upon thinking it over, had realized his identity; but Phillips had denied this, and there was no reason why he should lie. It would be hard for Karl Lewis, knowing his own guilt, to believe that Phillips had been drawn to the cottage by nothing more than the desire to talk to a pretty girl. The only remaining possibility, Phillips realized, was for him, Hugh Phillips, to have discovered something left behind by Janice. . . . It was as if a door at the back of his mind had opened, letting in a cold draft of fear. The tall man was after something that did not exist. Janice had not left anything. But there would be no way of convincing Karl Lewis. . . .

The tall man was staring down at him, blue-eyed and expressionless. Slowly his left hand found a pack of cigarettes in the pocket of the gray suit, shook one up, put it between his lips, and lit it with a silver lighter after putting the pack away.

"That's better," he said, reading something in the younger man's face of which Phillips himself was not aware. He blew out the flame, closed the cover, and dropped the lighter into his pocket. "Listen, kid," he said in a friendly voice. "Listen, Janey wrote me a letter. She wanted five thousand. She always was a greedy little tramp. . . ."

Phillips moved a little. Even if you had not got along too well with your wife, it was not pleasant to hear another man refer to her as a tramp. It reminded you that the other man had known her too well. He looked at Karl Lewis's face, trying to understand why the girl who had married him should have wanted to live with this man with the long hard face and the blue eyes that looked dead, like blue marbles. Or why the other girl should be willing to help him commit murder.

". . . I knew she'd be around for more later," Karl Lewis was saying. "She knew I'd killed a man in Hollywood on a little deal about whiskey for the club. . . . But you know all about that. She lost her nerve after giving me an alibi. I looked for her and couldn't find her. After a while I figured she was going to keep quiet, anyway, and I stopped looking. Then this letter, see?"

Phillips licked his lips. 'Did she say she was leaving a . . . ?"

". . . I sent one of the boys ahead before I mailed the money," the tall man went on, unheeding. "He picked her up in the Baltimore post office when she came for it and tailed her down here. . . . No, she hadn't said anything about leaving a note, or I wouldn't have . . . I thought she figured that being three thousand miles away she was safe. If she was leaving something around, to be delivered if anything happened to her, she'd have told me, wouldn't she? It wasn't any protection if I didn't know about it."

His voice was suddenly indignant, as if he were accusing Janice of playing him a trick. Phillips watched him uncomprehendingly; it seemed as if the tall man, after proving that Janice had left a note, was now busy proving the reverse.

"But in that case what makes you think . . . ?"

Karl Lewis looked up sharply. "You're here, aren't you? With this." He tapped the gun scornfully. "How would you know so much if she hadn't . . . ?"

Phillips opened his mouth and closed it again. The tall man was not talking to him, but to the girl, defending himself against the charge of having bungled the murder. He was not proving that no note existed, but merely that he could not have foreseen its existence.

"So I went ahead," Karl Lewis said. "Then I decided I'd better look through the house to make sure. . . ."

"Why didn't you take the picture and the bank book?" He could feel the rough flesh inside his lip where it had been cut against his teeth, and he knew that he hated the man who had struck him, the man who had lived with

Janice before he knew her. But there was no time for hatred.

Karl Lewis shrugged his shoulders. "I didn't know if you'd seen them, kid," he said. "I didn't want you to miss anything." He looked at the younger man for a moment. "And it wasn't there, was it? I was looking in the wrong place, wasn't I, kid?"

"It wasn't anywhere," Phillips said. "She didn't leave anything."

Karl Lewis smiled slowly. He spoke as if he had not heard. "So now . . ." he murmured, ". . . so now you'll get on the phone and call her, huh? Tell her to bring it with her."

Phillips looked up abruptly, for a startled moment thinking the other had gone mad and had forgotten that Janice was dead and who had killed her. Then he understood and felt panic grip his throat and stomach like the first pangs of seasickness. He was on his feet, and the tall man had taken a step backward, leveling the gun.

"Call who?" Phillips whispered.

"The girl," Karl Lewis said gently. "The girl you've been covering up for all evening, kid. The girl you've been trying to make us believe thinks you killed Janey."

Phillips whispered, "You're crazy. She doesn't . . ."

"You kind of overplayed that hand," the tall man said. "The minute you said that, about her accusing you of murder, I started wondering why you'd want to make so damn sure we didn't connect her with you."

"She hasn't anything to do with this," Phillips said breathlessly. "She thinks I . . ."

". . . killed Janey." Karl Lewis laughed. "Yeah, I know. I heard you the first time; remember, I was in the bedroom there? But it stinks, kid. It stinks. Janey left it with her, didn't she? You were Janey's husband, and she didn't want you to get curious about where she'd come from or why she'd want to leave a note like that. She couldn't be sure you wouldn't peek, eh, kid? But this girl, Christine, she'd recognized Janey, you said, and Janey made her promise to keep her trap shut. So maybe one of the boys wasn't as careful as he might have been, and

Janey recognized him and knew I was getting close to her, so she wrote something and left it with this girl who already knew all about her and wasn't going to tell. And tonight the girl, Christine, brought it to you and you got your gun and came over here—"

"No!"

"I say yes, kid. And don't try to tell me she's taken it to the cops, because if she had why should you think up a fancy story to keep her out of it? She'd be safe with the cops."

"She doesn't know anything about it," Phillips whispered. He could hear his own voice far away. It sounded ragged.

The tall man paid no attention to the interruption. "You figured you could come here and see what you could find out and if anything went wrong I wouldn't dare touch you because your girl had the evidence. Well, listen, little boy, I've had that gag pulled on me before. So now you'll call her and tell her everything's okay and the sheriff man, Holt, wants her to bring it right away . . . ."

A long time ago, before the war, they had gone down to the pier after two hot sets of tennis. They had stood on the pier, cooling off, and he had looked at her, seeing her flushed and warm and smiling and happy. He had known that he was in love with her. There were times when you knew a thing like that so sharply that you had to do something about it; and if the girl were like Chris, so that you could not grab her and kiss her in full daylight in front of God and everybody, you pushed her in the drink.

She made a beautiful splash and he watched her come up, her hair streaming down her face; then, to make a joke of it, suddenly embarrassed, he dove over her head into the water. She was pulling herself up the ladder, pushing back her hair, when he rose. *That was silly,* she gasped. *What if I'd had my watch on?* But she was laughing, and he could not, and did not want to, help seeing the way the wet tennis suit betrayed her fine body; and the way her arms and legs were golden in the sunlight. Perhaps she knew what he was thinking, because as he swam up she put a rubber-soled sneaker against his head and pushed him under. . . .

"No," he said.

The tall man struck him with the gun and he fell to the rug. He waited for the man to hit him again, and he knew that he was afraid, no longer of what the man might do to him, but that he might not be able to stand it; that he would call and Chris would come and he would have done this to her, too, as well as what he had done to her a year ago when he married Janice. He felt Karl Lewis approach. The man's foot caught him in the ribs and drove the breath out of him.

He closed his eyes tightly and watched the red spots dance through the blackness and waited for the blackness to become complete. Far away he heard a telephone dial clicking rhythmically. He wondered if he were really feeling the rug under his fingers, or if he were actually at the end of the room, doing what Karl Lewis wanted him to do. The thought drove him back to consciousness. He sat up.

XII

The girl he had known as Shirley Carlson leaned against the wall by the telephone table, running the fingers of her right hand through her already disheveled hair, while she listened to the instrument ringing in her ear. She looked up as Karl Lewis took a threatening step toward her and gestured him into silence. She shook her hair back from her face and stepped free of the wall, and suddenly she was a different person.

"Miss Wells? Miss Wells, this is Dr. Carlson's nurse." Her voice was precise and faintly accented with refinement. "Yes, Dr. Lewis Carlson. I am speaking from a cottage on Polling Creek, the last house on the road. You know where it is? It is called the Brown cottage, I think. . . . Yes, that is correct."

You could almost hear the starch on her uniform rustle as she looked up, facing the tall man over the telephone, defying him to snatch it away from her as he clearly wanted to.

"Yes," she said. "Yes, that's right. Yes . . ." Her voice became severe. "Miss Wells, if you'd allow me to go on. . . . We have a young man here. His boat capsized on the bay and the doctor was called. . . . Phillips. Yes, he is alive. . . ."

She waited, listening. Then she glanced up at the man standing over her, and a queer little half-triumphant smile came to her face and vanished.

"I *see,* Miss Wells," she murmured at last. "Yes, there was a question. . . . . You say his wife was killed in an accident and he . . . Yes, of course we noticed the bandage on his head. No, the doctor has not yet notified the police. Under the circumstances . . . I realize that, Miss Wells. As I was about to say, under the circumstances perhaps the doctor would be willing . . . Perhaps if you came out here, Miss Wells. He is asking for you. You're very welcome."

She hung up very gently and leaned against the wall, looking up at Karl Lewis. Her small face was suddenly drawn and tired, so that the color put into her face by the drinks she had taken looked unhealthy. When she spoke her voice was her own.

"She thinks he tried to commit suicide. She doesn't want us to call the police."

The tall man started to speak, but the girl suddenly swung herself away from him and walked quickly across the room to the liquor cabinet, a little unsteadily, the full black skirt bunching about her knees.

"He was telling the truth, Karl," she said thinly. "She does think he killed his wife. So now where are you?"

Karl Lewis said harshly, "She was kidding you. And if she thinks he killed his wife, why . . . ?"

"She's in love with him, you damn fool," the girl said without turning. "Some people don't seem to give a damn who a man kills. . . . Where the hell are the cigarettes? I haven't smoked for three weeks, playing your sissy daughter, and I'm going nuts. . . ." She tossed off a drink and shuddered.

"I don't want you too drunk to drive."

"I'm never too drunk to drive," the girl said, whirling. "Give me some cigarettes, damn you. . . ."

The tall man threw them to her. She picked them off the floor. Karl Lewis said, "You aren't taking a screen test, Kitten, so drop the Bette Davis."

The girl said in a low, intense voice, "She wasn't kidding me. They don't kid that good, darling. And he was telling the truth all along. He just came around for a shoulder to cry on. . . . And what are you going to do now? She's coming. I couldn't have stopped her, she'd have got suspicious. And *you* wanted to have him call her with that fairy tale about some note that doesn't exist!"

"But he came here," the tall man said. "I don't like that kind of coincidence."

"Coincidence?" The girl's laugh rose to a high musical note and seemed to ring through the room even after she had stopped laughing. The tall man whirled on Phillips, who had pulled himself up to the davenport.

"You don't move!" he said. "I don't want any trouble from *you!*"

"Coincidence!" the girl cried. "You brought him here. I brought him here. If we'd just pulled out after she was dead instead of hanging around to make sure. . . . But no, you had me go and be nice to him, to find out what he knew. And his girl thought he was a murderer, so he came here because I was such a nice girl—I can be a damn nice girl, you know, when I try—and he wanted somebody to talk to. Just like he said. And if you hadn't tried to be so bright we'd be back in Hollywood. . . ."

"With a gun?" the tall man said. "Would he have brought a gun?"

"Maybe something scared him. Maybe he was using it for a paddle. He brought it. And he was embarrassed as hell about it. You saw him. . . . Anyway, she thought he'd tried to commit suicide, and that means she thinks he's a murderer, so there goes your pipe-dream about any letter that woman left with her. If she'd seen any letter she'd know he wasn't a murderer, wouldn't she? So now what are you going to do with the two of them? Kill them, too?"

"Shut up," Karl Lewis said. "Shut up, Kitten." But she did not shut up, she kept right on talking.

It was, Hugh Phillips thought, like being in a cage with two bickering wild animals that had forgotten him for the moment; then the tires of a car scattered the gravel of the drive and put an end to it.

The car rushed to a halt outside. Chris's footsteps were running toward the porch before the door had time to slam shut behind her. Phillips heard them on the steps. Then there was a pause, and he could visualize her touching her hair, or smoothing her dress, or simply drawing a long breath that she had not had time for since the telephone rang, so that she would not betray herself too completely to the people in the house. She knocked twice on the screen.

He got up and walked slowly across the room toward the door.

He felt, but did not turn to see, the tall man's gun rise and steady behind him; he heard Shirley Carlson's breath catch in an audible gasp. There was in his mind the vague thought that if the gun went off, Chris might have time to turn and flee, but the two men waiting outside would probably catch her.

Suddenly he found himself facing the bitter realization that he had been uselessly brave and very stupid. If he had called her, telling her what Karl Lewis had wanted him to say, she might have thought he was crazy, but she would have guessed that he was in serious trouble, and she would probably have called the police. The girl had known. Shirley Carlson had realized that he had been telling the truth throughout, that Chris knew nothing, and that he must not be allowed to call her.

The gun did not go off. He heard Karl Lewis follow him across the room. He stopped at the door and felt the revolver touch him in the back. He looked up and saw Chris watching him through the screen door.

He knew that he did not look like a man who had been rescued from drowning. His clothes were dry, and he did not think there was blood on his face, or any mark that would be visible in the dim light on the porch. He was not obviously ill, nor did he seem to be receiving medical attention. Her eyes studied him carefully and something went out of them, sympathy perhaps, and bewilderment and a trace of fear took its place. She glanced at the two people behind him and pulled the door open and stepped up to the porch.

"Hello, Hugh," she said carefully.

"Hi, Chris."

She was still dressed in the white playsuit with the skirt that buttoned on to make a sports dress of it; it was crushed and wrinkled and her hair was not smooth. She was no longer wearing the black velvet band. He had not seen Chris look sloppy since they were kids. Her face was painfully clean and she had no lipstick on.

He knew as if he had been there that she had not been to bed, although it was past two in the morning. He knew that she had been lying on the bed, fully dressed, perhaps still crying a little, perhaps with all the tears out of her, staring at the ceiling; or perhaps she had been asleep at last, surprised to find herself so, when the telephone rang. She had taken the message and washed her face hastily and come here without stopping to change her dress or even put on lipstick.

He felt no sense of elation at knowing that what she believed about him had touched her so deeply; he could only feel a piercing sense of guilt at seeing her like that, rumpled and untidy and tired; because it was all part of the thing he had brought into their lives when, searching for a nameless excitement, he had married Janice. He felt the presence of the man with the china-blue eyes behind him, and the gentle touch of the gun in his back. He remembered that it was his own gun, and that it had a very long barrel.

"You'd better come in, Chris," he said.

Speaking, he swung his arm backward with a helpless desperation that was not courage but simply a refusal to stay alive and take the responsibility for what was going to happen to her at the hands of Janice's murderer.

He felt the barrel of the revolver against his wrist and the blast from the cylinder scorched him and he was not dead. He was pushing and kicking, shoving death back into the cottage, and closing the door on it; and he had not been able to get his hands on the gun but neither had the tall man been able to turn the unwieldy weapon against him. The gun crashed again inside. The bullet removed two panes of glass and the wood between them. He was running across the porch, seeing Chris's face wide-eyed and unbelieving, staring at him. He pushed her; she stumbled on the steps and went to her knees at the bottom; two men were coming up the bank from the drive at a run.

He heard the voice of the snub-nosed girl inside: "You damn fool, what do you think you're doing with that cannon? They can hear you clear to Baltimore!"

And the voice of the blue-eyed man, more clearly, as if the door had been opened. "Don't shoot, grab them. Head them off from the cars."

Chris was running across the unkempt lawn toward the bluff and he was following her. There were no more shots behind them. He had no hope that the shots that had already been fired would bring help; this was out in the country and some farmer was always letting off at crows or stray dogs: two shots meant nothing to anybody. They were only enough that the tall man would have to be conservative from now on; he could not afford to draw attention with a fusillade, now that people in the neighborhood might have been partially awakened. Chris saw the stairs and veered toward them and plunged down the long flight, her thin skirt ballooning about her knees. The slight wind caught at her hair and dress as she reached the dock. Phillips heard the heavy shoes of the men behind them on the stairs.

Then they were in the boat and he was paddling desperately with the single paddle while Chris, forward, hauled up the mainsail, and he heard himself laughing.

Chris said breathlessly, "Watch it, Hugh. Stop it! Take in on the mainsheet."

He glanced back. One of the men had reached the end of the dock and was aiming a gun at them, but the experimental way in which he held the weapon told that he did not intend to fire. But there was a strange fascination in watching a man debating with himself whether he should try to kill you or not. Then the gun dropped and the man turned back and joined the second man at the outboard runabout chained to the dock.

Chris pleaded, "Hugh . . . !"

He watched her rise to clear the jib as he sheeted in the mainsail and felt it fill. He steered and watched her get the jib up and turn, hampered by her skirt, to climb over the centerboard trunk; she snatched at the hem of her skirt with both hands and two buttons yielded with immense reluctance; sobbing a little, breathlessly, she gave it up, rammed the centerboard down, and dove for the trailing jibsheet, whipped into lazy snakelike patterns by the flapping sail.

"Watch it, Hugh," she gasped. *"Please* watch it. You're luffing."

He wanted to tell her not to work so hard. Behind them the men, seeing how funny it was, had stopped hurrying. One was walking deliberately along the shore toward the sandbar. He could wade out there and force them to stand well over to the far bank to avoid him. He did not have to walk fast. Even strolling along, watching them, he was already well ahead of them. Phillips thought he was grinning.

Karl Lewis was climbing back up the stairs to get the key for the runabout. The girl was nowhere in sight.

The sailboat heeled gently and gracefully and little ripples played along the planking and it was all very silly and futile. In a wind like this they would do two knots to windward; out on the bay, running free, they might do four or five; the runabout could probably do thirty.

Chris, lying flat on the weather deck to offer as little

resistance to the wind as possible, turned her head sharply.

"Hugh, you're sailing very badly. There isn't any wind ahead. Let's come about."

He remembered how, before the war, she had often crewed for him in races; and thought that he must really be horsing it up when Chris Wells could bring herself to tell him how to sail his own boat.

"All right," he said docilely, "ready about. Hard alee."

The little boat swung noiselessly. There was an infuriating leisureliness about it, as if they had all the time in the world. As if internal combustion engines had never been invented and death were a million miles away. The boat swung, the sails shivered a little and settled over on the new tack, the lines creaked and hardened, and they could hear again the little tinkling sounds of their progress through the dark, barely ruffled water. Directly ahead they could see the opening to the bay between the high shores, and the man waiting in ankle deep water at the edge of the reeds.

"Anyway," Phillips said dryly, "Anyway, there isn't any moonlight. Not that I can see how it helps."

Chris whispered, "Hugh, what is it? Who are they? Are they policemen?"

For a moment he could not speak, he could only look at her in amazement. Her face was a dim oval in the darkness, turned toward him over her shoulder. Even in the darkness he could see the sun-bleached streaks in the rumpled hair.

"I forgot," he said harshly. "No, they're not policemen, Chris. He's the man who killed Jan. Karl Lewis."

He thought she became pale, but he could not be sure. Then she turned her face abruptly away from him with a little gasp.

The boat slipped softly through the water toward the spit where the man was waiting. As it approached, he walked gingerly out until he was standing knee deep twenty yards from shore. They were heading directly for him, and the wind, slanting into the mouth of Polling Creek, would not let them point up farther toward the south bank to avoid him. The man began to wade to meet them, but the sandbar dropped off abruptly, wetting him to the waist, and he scrambled back to higher ground. He was a big man and he was holding in his hand, not a gun, but a short club, like a policeman's billy. Apparently Karl Lewis had decided to capture them alive. Later they would presumably be found drowned, washed up along the shore somewhere with the overturned sailboat.

Behind them the tall man had come down to the pier again. They heard the distant rattle of a chain, removed and thrown to the weathered boards.

"Ready about," Phillips whispered. "Hard alee."

They swung through an angle of ninety degrees and headed across the creek on the port tack, sailing parallel to the sandbar. Several boat-lengths to the left the big man splashed noisily abreast of them, saying nothing, keeping between them and the bay. He seemed gradually to diminish in size. When the water reached his chest he stopped, watched them sail on toward the darkness under the south bank, swore, and surged back toward shore. Phillips waited until he had covered half the distance; then came about again.

The man looked back, seemed about to return to intercept them as they sailed across the shallows toward open water, shook his head disgustedly, and plunged ashore. They could hear his shoes making sucking sounds in the muck among the reeds. He was running to catch the others before they shoved off. An outboard motor coughed twice and was silent. Chris giggled.

"Wouldn't it be funny—" She stopped and took the shrill note out of her voice. "Wouldn't it be funny if they couldn't start it?"

Outboard motors never started. You cranked them all around the bay and the river and they never started. It was an old joke. It was no good. The motor spluttered again, ran for a moment and was silent, but the joke was still no good.

Phillips crouched to look back under the sail, but the reeds had slipped astern of them to hide the dock. The boat was lifting and pitching, heeling to the fresh bay breeze. He caught his breath sharply: as they were sailing now, the sail hid them from shore. Back on the dock, the tall man, looking over the reeds to seaward, would be seeing nothing but a dim leaning sickle of sail standing out into the darkness.

Phillips wound the end of the mainsheet around the tiller and made it fast, adjusting it carefully. Then he sat quite still, watching the boat sail herself with the helm lashed half a point to starboard. He moved his tongue over his lips and looked at Chris. Her eyes widened a little with understanding, and she nodded. The boat lurched a little and she was gone. He saw her head rise astern. He had a momentary impulse to keep sailing, drawing the others away from her while she swam ashore; but he knew she would not stand for it and the boat would do the job for the two of them. He made a last minor adjustment of the tiller lashing and dropped over the side.

The water closed over him, not as cold as he had expected. He felt a moment of complete panic as his shoes and clothes seemed to drag him endlessly down through the murky water; he stroked once and felt the surface and opened his eyes and breathed. The boat was sailing rapidly away from him, leaving a slight phosphorescence in its wake. Lacking the weight of two people on deck, it was heeling quite sharply and, as Phillips watched, it nosed up into the wind, hesitated, fell off again, and sailed on. Already he could not read the name on the transom.

Chris's head broke water beside him. "Are you all right, darling? I can . . ."

"I'm fine," he said. "Let's get the hell out of here."

They had reached the shallows when the runabout came out. They crouched in the water and watched it roar past after the small unguided sail holding out into the bay; the runabout planing, flinging aside a curling bow wave and dragging a plume of roiled water astern. The sound of the motor was a shrill racketing whine. The wake hissed through the reeds toward them and washed over them, gritty with sand and covered with a scum of the small dead stuff that piled up against a lee shore. They scrambled into the reeds and crouched in the mud, listening to the sound of the motor.

"There were only two," Chris whispered. "Where's the third?"

There had been only two men in the boat, and neither had seemed to have gray hair, although it had been hard to tell in the darkness.

Phillips turned to look bleakly at the girl beside him, sitting among the roots of the reeds with her muddy hands held awkwardly away from her wet clothes. She looked away from him and began gingerly to unfasten her clinging skirt, peeling it away from her legs. He crouched beside her in the darkness, knowing that neither of them had the courage to leave the shelter of the reeds. Karl Lewis might be standing just outside, waiting. He might have turned their own trick back on them, sending the runabout after a boat he knew to be empty, as a blind to cover his own approach.

Out on the water the sound of the outboard motor lost a couple of octaves in pitch. Phillips did not raise himself to look. It was easy enough to know what was happening out there; the runabout had reached the empty sailboat and was slowing to examine it. The men in the speedboat would have to come close to make sure that no one was lying down in the cockpit.

Then footsteps stopped at the edge of the reeds. The sound of the motor came back to its former pitch and volume—the speedboat turning back; and the reeds whispered protestingly as Karl Lewis came forward through the mud to meet it.

Phillips felt Chris close beside him and, glancing aside, dimly saw her pressing herself down among the springy stalks as he was doing, her body stiff with revulsion at the cold seeping wetness of the mud. She had twisted out of her sodden skirt, but even in the dark he could see that her playsuit was filthy; and as he stared at a black smear on the soaked white cloth of her sleeve, he remembered that he had seen all this before. Once before he had lain helpless, watching a girl in a white dress be killed.

He groped cautiously among the stalks of the reeds, seeking a weapon, a piece of driftwood, a stone, anything he could throw or strike with. His fingers found only the slippery folds of Chris's discarded skirt, half buried in the muck: then the tall form of the blue-eyed man was above him and the world was a very small place, holding three people and the sound of an outboard motor. As he rose he noticed with a thin flash of amusement that the tall man was now carrying his own gun.

Karl Lewis started and turned as he lunged forward; and he knew a thrust of hope; the other had not guessed the trick, did not yet quite understand that the boat had been empty, was not expecting attack here on shore. His gun went off prematurely as Phillips dragged the wet cloth out of the mud, hearing mud and water sluice from it in a wide arc as he swung. The cloth opened in the air and he cracked it like a whip; the tall man threw himself back to avoid it, but it wound itself around his head in thin adhesive folds. The gun went off again, blindly. Phillips followed the tall man backward, reaching for the weapon; it crashed a third time as they fell; and he felt the altered concussion of a fourth discharge and knew that the automatic, choked with mud, had exploded.

The body beneath him twisted and squirmed and, sobbing for breath, he reached for the throat and hung on. A hand came up to beat at his face and he gagged and hid his face against the other's chest, because the hand was ragged and incomplete, shattered by the explosion of the pistol. The broken hand tried to claw away the slippery folds that muffled the face, and the fingers crushing the throat.

Phillips heard the steady approaching whine of the outboard motor over the surging of blood in his ears. Then it changed pitch, and he knew the speedboat was turning away. Chris screamed sharply once, and was silent. None of it was particularly important. He would find out what it all meant when the man he was choking was dead.

A hand touched his shoulder. He looked up into the dark face of the black-haired man named Holt.

"All right, kid," Mr. Holt said. "Give him air. We'll take care of him from here."

XIII

He could trace in his mind the steps by which he had got from Polling Creek to the guest room at the Wellses', and all the time he had been thinking that if they wouldn't talk so much and would move faster instead of standing around talking, he might possibly hang on long enough to get cleaned up and in bed before he blacked out completely. But when the doctor turned out the light and left him alone he lay staring up at the dark ceiling, watching the patterns of light shift as cars came and went in the drive. He waited for the shutter to close on his consciousness, but he had been holding it open too long. The damn thing was stuck.

At last he switched on the light again and sat up, clumsily lighting a cigarette from a package somebody had left under the lamp on the bedside table. He rubbed the aching welt along his jaw where the tall man had struck him with the gun-barrel, and smoked, and looked around the room, having seen it a hundred times before. Whenever Sand Point became crowded with guests, before the war, he would be sent over here with his pajamas and toothbrush. When the Wellses were hard up for room, Chris would come to Sand Point to sleep on the sunporch.

The room was at the rear of the house. The bathroom was opposite the stairs; then there was Chris's room and the big front bedroom overlooking the bay. He knew the house as well as he knew Sand Point and it should have felt almost like being home, but instead it made him feel restless and unhappy. He had no right here; he was trading on something he had had once and had thrown away.

Nobody seemed to be upstairs. They were all down below, talking. Then he heard footsteps that he recognized, coming up.

She hesitated at the head of the stairs, came to the door, and opened it cautiously. He saw that she had got some of the mud off her, but not all; her grimy white playsuit looked almost dry, but her hair was still damp, and she looked terribly tired. He was suddenly glad for all the talk; she had heard everything, there was nothing he needed to explain to her. She knew about the tall man, and how she had come to be called; and she even knew about the girl. He did not even have to explain to her how he had felt about Janice, because she had known it before he did. There was nothing to explain, and there was really not very much to say.

"You're supposed to be asleep, Hugh," she said. "Do you want me to get the doctor to give you something before he goes?"

"No, I'm all right," he said. "You'd better get something dry on, hadn't you?"

"I'm going to," she said. ". . . The doctor said you should stay in bed at least ten days. He says your headaches are due to concussion from the accident. . . . Didn't they tell you when you left the hospital that you should stay quiet?"

"They always tell you that."

"Mother called your folks," she said. "They'll be down in the morning."

"Fine."

"Well," she said, "well, I'm going to take a bath. You'd better turn out the light and try to sleep."

"I will as soon as I've finished this smoke."

She looked at him for a moment, and her mouth had suddenly a tight, almost frightened look. He thought he knew how she felt. It was hard to realize that a person you had known very well once could have become almost a stranger, that you could not talk to. She turned quickly and went out, closing the door quietly behind her.

He pushed the pillow up behind his shoulders and

leaned against the head of the bed and stared blankly at the curling smoke of the cigarette. He tried to think what was in her mind and in his own, but he could not feel anything but a vague tired bitterness. He did not blame her for anything. The war was still close enough that you remembered that almost anybody, given an opportunity and an excuse, would kill: it did not anger him that she had thought him a murderer. But the fact that she could think so, and that they had not even been able to talk it out between them, showed how far apart they had come in a year.

He found himself almost wishing for Janice. Janice had been like the little girl who was horrid when she was bad, but when she was good she was very, very good. . . . And at any rate he had known her, and could talk to her. Then he realized that even this was not true and he had no idea what the real Janice had been like. The tall man had called her a greedy little tramp. The tall man had probably never chased fireflies with her. . . . He had lived a year with a woman who had not existed. And the long-legged girl with the upturned nose, whom he had kissed, had not existed, either. Everybody was six other people.

Mr. Holt opened the door gently, looked inside, and came in. There was mud on his shoes and on the cuffs of his trousers, but he looked satisfied with the world. He stood over the bed, studying Hugh Phillips's face, and misinterpreted the expression he found there.

"You're still pretty sore at me, aren't you, Mr. Phillips?"

Phillips shook his head.

Mr. Holt asked quietly, "How do you think we happened to be there? We've been watching the place for a week. The man on the job tonight missed you because he wasn't expecting anybody coming by water; but when he saw the young lady drive in, he knew that something was up and passed the word along. . . ."

"Then you knew all the time. . . ."

The black-haired man drew up a chair and sat down.

"Could I miss it?" he asked. "I said to myself, hell, the boy's crazy; and then I looked at her head. . . ."

Phillips winced. "Yes," he said slowly. "I thought of that. It made me wonder if I hadn't been dreaming."

"I had a time with the doctor," Mr. Holt said, smiling. "He wanted to spill it; I had to swear I'd give it out in a week no matter what happened; and that the coroner wouldn't ask any leading questions. When the week was up . . . Mr. Phillips, I've been busy as a three-legged dog with fleas, and that damn doctor like to climb down my throat. . . ."

Phillips crushed out his cigarette in the glass ashtray on the bedside table.

"I still don't get it," he said, and he knew that his voice was unfriendly. "Suppose you had let me tell it. With the doctor's evidence, certainly I'd have been believed. . . ."

"Mr. Phillips, you should know something about politics." The black-haired man smiled cheerfully. "Look, Mr. Phillips, there's an election coming up . . . and you come along, yelling murder. Sure it was murder. But my God, did you have to call a plain old socket wrench what you did?"

"What difference—?"

"The Black Cross!" said Mr. Holt with a wry grimace. " 'My wife was killed by a man wielding a black cross.' And the wounds in her head to prove it! Can't you see the reporters diving for the phone booths? Hell, they'd have had the Black Hand, the KKK, and the Spanish Inquisition, all loose in this County together. I wouldn't wonder but some of them would have made a swastika of it and claimed the old man was hiding Nazis under his bed. . . . Don't you see, Mr. Phillips? I had to stop it. I had to give myself time to work on it. Now we can break it all together and what you said doesn't make any difference. They can't let their imaginations loose on it because we'll give them the answer before they can get started. They can't make anything of it that isn't there."

"Yes," said Phillips grimly. "But you might have let me in on it."

Mr. Holt grinned. "I figured I'd better let you stew a while, Mr. Phillips, seeing as I wasn't at all sure you hadn't used the wrench on her yourself."

Phillips started. Then he laughed. "Yes, I kind of wondered if you . . . But how would I have got rid of it?"

The older man said calmly, "The girl might have got rid of it for you. When I saw the two of you leaving the inquest together I was mighty glad I hadn't let on to you."

"I'd never seen her in my life, before . . ."

"Was I going to take your word for that, Mr. Phillips? After all, men have been known to get rid of their wives before, when someone else came along. When I checked on her, though, I found that she'd never been east of St. Louis before. She'd gone to Hollywood from St. Louis for the same reason all of them go; and when she couldn't make the grade she got a job selling cigarettes at a place called the Grotto. Run by this man Lewis, who'd been mixed up in some things including a murder for which he'd been alibied by a young lady answering your wife's description, who'd later disappeared. When I found Mr. Lewis here, in the same cottage with the Carlson girl, things began to make sense, kind of. We were tracing the truck when you broke things up."

"Have you found it?"

The black-haired man shrugged. "We know where to look for it now. There were three men, claiming to be fishermen, living in a cottage down the road from the Brown place. One of them disappeared the night your wife was killed. The girl says he drove the truck west and gave us some ideas where we might find him. She's down town making a statement now. We caught her trying to get away while the men were after you and Miss Wells."

Phillips said, "Yes, she was getting pretty close to a breakdown."

Mr. Holt rose. "I tell you, Mr. Phillips," he said, and suddenly his face looked tired, "I tell you, I hate a case where a nice-looking girl is involved. Half the time you'll give her breaks you wouldn't give a man, and the other half you'll be harder on her than you would a man, to show you can't be influenced. I know. I was eight years on the force in Baltimore before I married and moved down here. . . ." He grimaced. "Hell, I've got a daughter fifteen who wants to go to Hollywood. Why can't they stay home?"

Hugh Phillips regarded the strong mahogany face of the black-haired man curiously. In the hospital Mr. Holt had been an impressive figure who had spoken to him convincingly from the heights of a superior strength and wisdom, calling him 'kid.' That was the way Phillips had remembered him, with a certain amount of antagonism, but also with something very close to fear. But tonight Mr. Holt had become, suddenly, merely a large weathered man who still knew things that Hugh Phillips did not know, but who addressed him respectfully with a distinct country accent, and asked for his sympathy and understanding. He was another person who was six other people.

It occurred to Phillips that Mr. Holt was a very good actor and something of a diplomat; he was, in other words, a politician. In the hospital he had wanted Phillips's silence and had obtained it by a shrewd mixture of bluff, veiled threats, and downright lies. Now he needed Phillips's cooperation and was willing to become a likeable yokel to get it: even though the case had closed favorably, Mr. Holt had no desire to have the bereaved husband complaining that he had been browbeaten into concealing his wife's murder for political reasons.

"Well," Phillips said slowly, when the other did not speak. "Well, any way you want to handle it, Mr. Holt. . . . All I want to do is forget about it." After all, the man had done a good job and had probably saved his life. Although one could not help wondering just how far Mr. Holt would have got had Karl Lewis not sent the girl to pick up Phillips after the inquest. . . .

The room seemed to change when he was gone, as if he had taken with him the world in which people murdered, were murdered, were suspected of murder; the world in which the policeman was not an automaton at a street crossing, but a central fact of life. Phillips moved after a while, reaching for the light switch. Then he let his hand fall slowly, and lighted a fresh cigarette; and after a long time, as he had hoped she would, seeing the light under his door, she came.

It was not quite fair of him, he thought, to have been married. He knew a little too much. He was quite aware of how hard she must have worked to get her hair looking so well so quickly; and after a year of marriage he could readily tell when a girl had taken pains with her make-up; and he knew that the pale blue printed satin housecoat she was wearing was a special one reserved for traveling or when there was company in the house, because a girl did not buy a thing like that just to have breakfast with her mother. He noticed these things and found that they gave him a little hope.

The housecoat made her, however, look quite tall and rather remote from anything he remembered about her.

"Why aren't you asleep?" she asked.

"I guess I wanted to see you."

He watched her come forward and sit down on the side of the bed. She smoothed the shining skirt of the housecoat over her knee and traced the pattern on it with her finger.

"I didn't think you would," she said at last.

"Would what?"

"Want to see me." He saw a slow flush rise under the golden sunburn of her face. "I don't know how I could have said something so . . . so completely dreadful. Even if I thought it I didn't have to say it. . . . But I couldn't stand it any longer. I had to know if you had killed her."

Her freshly washed hair curled, a little damp, at the nape of her neck behind her ear. He could see a small pulse beating inside the low collar of the coat.

"Chris," he said, "Chris, when that girl called you, and you thought I'd tried to commit suicide . . ."

She did not look up. "Oh, she told you."

"Yes. She said you asked her not to call the police. What were you going to do, Chris?"

"I don't know," she whispered.

"You thought I was a murderer. When Lewis shot at me you thought he was a policeman. But you ran with me; on the boat you were doing your best to help me get away. . . ."

Chris stood up suddenly and walked across the room to the dresser. He could see her face in the mirror; then she had turned abruptly to face him.

"It isn't quite fair to ask, is it, Hugh?" she said stiffly. "It makes me look rather like a fool, doesn't it?"

It had never occurred to him before that Christine Wells was beautiful. Perhaps he had never really looked at her before; he had known her too long. The discovery embarrassed him and he did not know how to behave. He thought of the year of their lives he had wasted.

"No," he said. "I'm the one who looks rather like a fool, Chris."

A BRAND NEW
MATT HELM
suspense novel

NAME: MATTHEW HELM

CODE NAME: ERIC

MISSION: #9 THE DEVASTATORS

REMARKS: On a bleak and lonely heath in northern Scotland they recovered the body of the third agent sent on this mission. He had died—been murdered—of bubonic plague. It was up to Matt Helm to take it from there. For somewhere among those desolate Scottish moors was a half-crazed scientific genius who could devastate entire populations with one hideous, raging plague. It was Helm's job to get him ... with the help of a beautiful American operative who was supposed to be his wife, and a beautiful Russian operative who made it clear she was his deadly enemy.

"Donald Hamilton's toughened secret agent Matt Helm never fails to pull off a first-rate adventure."
—The Hartford Courant

D1608   *A Fawcett* **Gold Medal Book**   **50¢**

On sale wherever paperback books are available